I0597559

Problem At the Park

Book Two in the Lemon Lister Mystery Series

By

Benna Bos

©2025 by Benna Bos
First publication 2025
Flashpoint Publications

All rights reserved. No part of this publication may be reproduced, transmitted in any form or by any means, electronic or mechanical, including photocopy, recording, or any information storage and retrieval system, without permission in writing from the publisher. Parts of this work are fiction. Names, characters, places, and incidents either are the product of the author's imagination or are used fictitiously, and any resemblance to actual persons, living or dead, business establishments, or events is entirely coincidental.

Paperback ISBN 978-1-61929-577-3
Hard Cover ISBN 978-1-61929-579-7
eISBN 978-1-61929-578-0

Cover Design by AcornGraphics

Publisher's Note:

The scanning, uploading, and distribution of this book via the Internet or via any other means without the permission of the publisher is illegal and punishable by law. Please purchase only authorized electronic editions, and do not participate in or encourage electronic piracy of copyrighted materials. Your support of the author(s)'s rights is appreciated.

Chapter One

Lemon waved the ugly, black lump in front of Milo's big nose. "See, yummy. Don't you want to search for these, buddy?"

Her hope skyrocketed the moment he lowered his head, ears dragging on the ground. His short legs carried his robust body across the grass, all of it following in the wake of his Basset Hound nose.

"That's right, Milo. Find the truffle, sweetie." Lemon hung onto the leash and waited for him to pull her toward the spot nestled beneath an olive tree where she'd stashed the other insanely expensive bit of fungus. "I spent a lot of money on these ugly little things, baby. So you should help mommy out and learn how to find them."

Milo continued his journey over the patch of ground at the edge of the Presidio. Lemon was certain the hound was unencumbered by her motives for this training session and driven only by his powerful nose. His legs marched on. The sudden tug on the leash yanked Lemon forward, catching her toe on a patch of rough ground. Gracelessly, she hit the stiff, dry grass typical of California fire season.

The leash slipped from her hand. It bounced across the field as Milo headed toward his goal. Lemon dragged herself to her feet and reached into her treat pouch. "Milo, I've got chicken liver. Don't go too far, buddy."

She headed toward the dog's long tail, stuck up in the air like a flag of triumph. No longer lumbering after his olfactory prize, Milo stayed in one place and pawed at something unseen.

Lemon glanced to her right, mentally waving at the abandoned truffle as she passed it to catch up with Milo. During her approach, a sickly scent wafted on the fog-dusted air. Lemon sighed, dropping her head in defeat.

"Again, Milo?"

The dog ripped his attention away from his find to gaze up at her, his jaw dropped open in his own special version of a smile. He panted and licked his lips. Lemon thought she saw pride sparkling in his big, brown eyes.

Lemon peeked around his squat body and cringed. Her own nose had nothing on Milo's, but it hadn't exaggerated about the state of the dead pigeon. "Really, dude?" Lemon grabbed Milo's leash and coaxed him away from his find. "This is exactly why we're doing this."

She moved toward the abandoned truffle, not about to leave such a valuable treat for their pigeon friend's mourners. "We gotta get you to find something other than dead stuff. My stomach can't take it anymore."

Lemon retrieved the fungus and held it in front of Milo. He turned away. "My man, this is way better than finding dead stuff. And if you learn how to find them, we can go up north and do some truffle hunting and make some money. That wouldn't be so bad, would it?"

Completely avoiding her, Milo panted, his gaze pointed toward the deceased bird. Lemon shoved both pieces of black gold in a paper bag and stuffed the whole thing in the pocket of her windbreaker. She headed toward the sidewalk, determined to find something better to do with the rest of her Saturday.

When she reached the crest of the hill, her phone vibrated against her belly. She slid down the zipper of her jacket and fumbled to reach into the internal pocket where she kept the thing. It continued to shake as she tugged and twisted to unlock it from its mesh and polyester cage.

The device finally stilled, but its incessant alerting meant someone was texting in small batches. Even before she lit up the screen, Lemon knew it had to be Mei. She glanced at the time on her lock screen. Lunch time.

Mei transferred over to the de Young Museum after a short, but exciting, stint at the Legion of Honor. So far her only complaint about the curatorial assistant job was the requirement of working weekends when Lemon didn't usually have any clients. Mei asked her regularly to change her schedule, citing that as a business owner, Lemon could set her own hours. But the high-end clientele she inherited wanted their dogs walked during banker's hours, and Lemon was at their mercy.

Lemon pulled up the texts and ran through them, her heartbeat increasing with each short line.

OMG

Cops might take my phone soon

Come here

Now please

Lemon pumped her legs. Her sneakers hit the concrete sidewalk as she sent back: *What is going on?*

Her head bounced up and down, shifting her gaze from the path home to the phone screen. But there was no reply.

Mei! Answer me.

Nothing. She and Milo approached the apartment her parents had given her before they escaped to a new life in Belize. She hated to tease her other two dogs, but she needed to drop off Milo and grab the keys to her van. She burst through the entrance, ran up the stairs, and entered her place in short order. As expected, Snickers and Klee both demanded a proper greeting.

Moving fast. As she unhooked Milo and gave out pats to the other two dogs as her mind traced the route she planned to take to Golden Gate Park that would lead her directly to the parking garage hidden beneath it with easy access to the de Young Museum.

Her phone rang during the hunt for her van keys. Practically tripping over an enthusiastic Klee, she managed to recover the phone and press the speaker button. "Hello? Mei?"

"No, Ms. Lister. It's Detective Zahn."

Lemon's heart sank. It wasn't that she didn't like the man, just the opposite in fact. But getting a call from a San Francisco homicide detective never resulted in a great day.

"Oh, hi Detective. What can I do for you?"

"Well, first, I want to let you know that I am with your friend, Mei, and she's okay."

Lemon's head swam in a thick soup of confusion and fear. "Okay."

"We're both hoping you are free to come down to Golden Gate Park to meet up with us." The detective threw out the statement as if it were an invitation to an afternoon tea party.

"Um, yeah. I can be there in about ten minutes, depending on parking."

"Don't worry about that. An officer will have a space held for you on the street in front of the museum. But I need you to bring the hound dog."

"Milo? You want me to bring Milo with me?"

"Yes. Absolutely. Please bring the dog."

Questioning authority sat low on Lemon's list of favorite things. It butted heads with her shy nature and her deeply ingrained insecurities. But words flew out of her mouth and overrode her inner introvert. "We're not really in the business of dead people anymore, detective. So—"

"I'll explain everything when you get here. See you in ten." The detective ended the call before Lemon could muster up more courage to challenge him.

She glanced at Milo, who lay settled into his fluffy dog bed, eyes firmly closed. "Sorry buddy. We gotta go."

Milo opened one eye and glared at her like a disgruntled pirate.

"Sorry. Looks like we have something unpleasant to do."

****

The police officer directed Lemon into the parking space at Fulton and tenth, his arms waving, his fingers curling and uncurling fast enough to blur. She managed to wedge the van between an electric car the size of a toaster and a boat-like sedan without too much trouble. As soon as she shoved the gearshift into park, Milo stirred. The hound lifted his head off the vinyl covering on the van's passenger seat and swung it to peer over at her.

She pulled the keys out of the ignition. "Let's go, pal."

Lemon hopped out of the van and rounded the vehicle to the passenger door. She yanked it open and coaxed Milo out of his warm, cozy seat. He begrudgingly allowed her to lift him down so she could set his wide paws on the concrete sidewalk.

"Ms. Lister, the detective is this way." The officer pointed toward the regal building housing the de Young Museum.

"Thanks." Lemon gripped the loop of Milo's leash and hurried toward the art museum's front entrance.

A sloping path wove through carefully planted flowers and delicate, low-lying bushes. A herd of children wearing identical blue vests stood in a noisy clump on her left. The sound of an adult counting heads was nearly drowned out by squeals of delight as Milo loped past on short legs carrying his bulky body in an always comical waddle.

As Lemon approached the large, glass doors signaling the entrance to the museum, another police officer intercepted them. He directed them around to the back, near the employee entrance where a concrete picnic table, tucked out of sight of the main entrance, held the petite body of Lemon's best friend.

Milo barked out a greeting. Mei, eyes wide and rimmed in red, ran at full speed toward Lemon. Despite her lingering fear of the big hound, Mei tossed herself into Lemon's arms, pressing her warm face into the crook of Lemon's neck.

"Are you okay?"

"No. This sucks." Mei pulled back and blinked her eyes. "I found a gun."

"Okay." While alarming, it was still a far cry from the craziest thing Lemon had ever found in the city. Granted, a disembodied foot tended to be high on the weird-o-meter.

"No, you don't understand. It's a cop gun." Mei wrung her hands together as Lemon realized the implication.

"Oh."

"Yeah. Oh."

"Ms. Lister." Detective Zahn approached their little klatch. "Good to see you again." He held out his hand. Lemon shook it, but there was no way she could honestly return the sentiment. Detective Zahn glanced down at Milo. His usually grumpy expression morphed into a crooked smile. "And you brought my main man, Milo."

"Yeah. But no body parts, right?"

"No. No. Just looking for any other possessions from Officer Hyatt."

And there it was, the inkling of an idea that formed in Lemon's mind when Mei said the gun belonged to a police officer. Now the sad truth was confirmed.

Like everyone else in the Bay Area, Lemon followed every crumb of information about the officer that went missing three days ago. Everyone on the SFPD was out looking for her.

Lemon turned to Mei. The incredulity in her voice reflected back to her. Why them? Six months ago Lemon—actually Milo—found a foot. Now Mei found the service weapon of a missing cop? What was it with the beings living at 3930 Arguello? Lemon asked Mei, "How did you find it?"

Shame colored Mei's face. "I was vaping again."

Lemon sighed. Sure, she hated when Mei took up vaping after quitting—something that happened in a regular six to eight week cycle. But Mei's weird habit of going to great lengths to hide it proved to be even more dangerous than inhaling toxic substances. In her attempts to find hidden cubie holes to sneak away to, she'd been locked in a creepy basement, nearly mugged in a sketchy alley, and once she used an old fire escape that she then became trapped on and the actual fire department had to come rescue her.

"So, you were hiding in the bushes."

Mei gazed off in the distance as she confirmed Lemon's suspicion. "Yep."

Detective Zahn seemed unfazed by Mei's antics. "If you would come this way please, Ms. Lister."

Lemon, with Milo at her side and Mei trailing behind, followed the detective into a thin strip of land squished between long, irregular rows of rough, wild-looking hedges. This section of the park was clearly never meant to be visited by tourists and pleasure-seekers.

They were not alone in the brush. A woman stood directly in their path with a stately German Shepard sitting pretty at her side. Her police uniform and the patch on her arm with the K-9 embroidered on it explained who she was, but not why she wore an expression of extreme annoyance.

"Officer Timkins. This is Lemon and her dog, Milo. The one I told you about."

The officer's frown deepened. Her hands remained wrapped tightly around the leather dog leash. "I don't see how that dog." She glanced down at Milo with pure disdain written on her face, "is going to be able to do what Lyka couldn't."

Unperturbed, Zahn shrugged. "Doesn't hurt to let him try."

"Maybe this isn't such a good idea." Lemon had to agree with the K-9 officer, With an actual trained dog on the scene, Lemon and Milo were out of their element. "I mean, Milo's past successes were a bit of a fluke."

"Nonsense. It can't hurt to try," Zahn said. "We have a missing officer to find. I will try anything."

"Okay. What are we supposed to do exactly?"

Officer Timkins stepped back, exposing a black gun that lay on the ground like an ominous harbinger of terror. "That's Officer Hyatt's service weapon. Have the dog sniff it, then follow the scent. If he can."

"Um, sure." Lemon said. Not at all certain how to make Milo do anything he didn't want to do, she held the leash up and pretended to possess a confidence that had never been in her personal toolkit.

"Go on, Milo," Mei encouraged from behind Lemon. "Sniff boy."

The eyeroll produced by Officer Timkins clearly projected her thoughts on their technique. "Really Zahn?"

Detective Zahn held up one hand. "I'm telling you, this boy is magic. He found a body in a stone sarcophagus."

"He got lucky." Timkins tone left little room for argument.

Lemon couldn't respond if she wanted to. Vibrating with nerves, she watched Milo's wet, brown nose stretch toward the gun. She attempted to will him to move closer, maybe even press that leathery organ against the steel to get a good whiff of the woman who owned it.

But he didn't. Milo stopped, whirled that powerful schnoz around, and loped in the opposite direction. When the slack was gone in his leash, he bolted forward, pulling Lemon behind him like a clumsy sled he was unwillingly attached to.

Chapter Two

Milo tugged at the leash. Lemon knew better than to resist. All sixty-five pounds of his low-slung body, when following a scent, was no match for her. That she stood on two legs and weighed over double what he did had no effect. Her arm jolted with the leash, nearly unbalancing her as Milo headed directly for the Japanese Tea Garden.

Lemon glanced back at her entourage. Surely heading into the popular tourist attraction on a Saturday with a determined Bassett Hound and a pack of police in tow was a bad idea. That trepidation grew as she quickly counted the hoard behind her. In addition to Mei, Detective Zahn, the grumpy K-9 cop, and her pup, the crowd included at least half a dozen uniformed police and a few more detectives in dark slacks and button-up shirts.

She swiveled her attention back to Milo. What would happen when they reached the ticketed entrance gate to the elegant gardens? The line of people waiting to pay snaked out onto the main path, the groupings of visitors like a set of bowling pins about to be clobbered by the giant clump of humans led by one big-eared dog.

Just before the imminent collision, Milo pivoted, his nose dragging them around the north end of Stow Lake. That route plunged them into a series of road crossings. Lemon's heart nearly stopped when the usually cautious Milo completely ignored the potential for danger and pounced toward the pavement.

Lemon was about to throw herself on the ground to halt his forward motion when one of the uniformed police officers saved her from that fate by jumping out ahead of them to stop traffic.

Once they were safely across the streets, Milo took them into the vast picnic area. For a terrifying moment, Lemon feared they would discover that his powerful olfactory organ led them to nothing more than lunch. But he ignored the groups of people picnicking and grilling and headed to Lindley Meadow.

That's when the hound finally slowed his pace, his signature gait returning as his squat body followed his big head across the grass. His audience slowed as well, the herd of people fanning out into a loose group, eyes scanning the ground.

"Lyka and I already searched this area," Officer Timkins said. "Zahn. This is crazy, following this animal around the park. If Lyka didn't find any—"

Zahn held up one hand like a stop sign. "Caroline. Relax."

Lemon focused on Milo's slow progress across the grass rather than the icy dialogue coming from the stressed out officers. Straight and narrow, but still slow and methodical, Milo's path led to a messy grove of trees and undergrowth. Thick and dark, it stood in contrast to the sun painted meadow.

The ground curved upward as they approached the trees. Lemon's legs strained. Milo panted. They reached the edge of the jumble of vegetation. Rather than pulling Lemon into the tangled mess, Milo carefully moved around the edge.

Musky, acrid, and metallic all at once, a horrific scent floated up and slammed into Lemon. She reeled backward. Milo lay down and whined.

"Oh God," Lemon said.

"Lyka detects something," Officer Timkins shouted.

"Ya think?" Zahn said. "We can all smell that."

Lemon dug her heels into the grass. "I think Milo and I are just gonna hang here."

"Yikes," Mei pulled up beside Lemon, nose scrunched up.

Zahn directed the officers. "Wilkins, Jamison. Go in carefully. Don't disturb anything, just confirm that I need to get forensics out here."

Two of the uniformed officers breached the edge of the trees and almost instantly disappeared in the thick branches. They returned moments later, both pale and sickly-looking. "Yeah. Boss. You better call."

****

Rarely did Lemon wish she had a full slate of dogs to walk. To bemoan the weekend was an odd sensation. But she would give any-thing to have an excuse to leave. Mei, whose interrupted workday pro-vided the perfect escape, instead stayed by Lemon's side, with the full permission of her boss, who like many other people had popped by to see what was going on behind the yellow police line.

"Do you think we really have to stay here?" Lemon's short hair blew into her eyes and back out again, the curls bouncing in the mild breeze.

Their little spot on the grass was just far enough away from the clump of woods to avoid the smell, and they purposely plopped, criss-cross applesauce, on the ground down wind of the decaying human body. Milo curled in a ball and snoozed away between them.

"Are you kidding? Why would you want to leave?" Mei pointedly looked at the police line their little spot sat within. On the other side, a crowd of looky-loos were gathered, their phones held up in what was obviously an attempt to get pictures.

"I'm kinda over dead bodies. In fact, I was never into them to begin with." Lemon glanced at the sleeping hound. "I was trying to teach him to hunt truffles when you had to go tromping through the bushes and find a gun."

"What can I say. Adventure awaits us."

"We have such different definitions of adventure."

"I know. We always have." Mei patted Lemon's knee and returned her attention to the gathering of law enforcement professionals. "Hey. CSI is here. You think Jade is coming?"

"Probably." Despite her casual tone, Lemon's stomach clenched.

"It's been a while since you broke up, have you seen her at all?" Mei asked.

"I told you, we didn't break up." It seemed no matter how many times she tried to explain what happened between her and Jade, Mei refused to hear it.

"Oh, right." Mei rolled her eyes. "You're just taking a break."

"We're exploring our future."

"By not hanging out."

"Exactly." Lemon knew that was as close as they would get to an understanding on the subject today. Mei and Lemon viewed their love lives in completely opposite ways.

"Speak of the devil."

Lemon followed Mei's pointing finger to find the tall, lean blonde ducking under the yellow tape, her dark blue coveralls a clear sign to the public that she was with the crime lab. Jade's ponytail swung violently as she marched over to the group of her colleagues. She approached a woman with bright red hair, the one who'd arrived on the scene first that afternoon.

"She looks pissed," Mei said.

"And she doesn't have her kit."

"Kit?"

"Yeah, you know, the big suitcase-y thing she carries to crime scenes. She had it with her at the Legion when Milo found the… you know."

Mei frowned at the sleeping dog. "You really like dead stuff, don't you dude?"

With the exception of his chest smoothly rising and falling, Milo didn't stir.

"He really does," Lemon lamented.

"Whoa."

Lemon followed Mei's gaze to Jade. She stood on the hill shaking her head, blonde locks dancing around her shoulders as she shouted something unintelligible at the red head. Then she pivoted on her heel.

Just as Lemon sent out a prayer to the universe that she and Mei were somehow invisible at the bottom of the hill, Jade's sharp eyes honed in on them. With her long legs covering a lot of ground quickly, she made her way to their refuge.

Lemon's mind scrambled as Jade approached. The last time they communicated was by text a week ago. The last time they spoke was by phone two weeks ago. And over a month had passed since they saw each other in person—an encounter far more awkward than Lemon cared to reveal to anyone, let alone Jade herself.

Lemon painted a smile on her face and occupied her hands by twisting them up in the leather leash. As Jade drew closer, her gaze trained on Milo, her expression became clear. Anger and pain warred for dominance on her delicate features.

"Hey, Jade," Mei said.

Jade dropped down on the grass on the other side of Milo and immediately reached out to stroke his short, multi-colored fur. "Hey."

"You okay?"

Jade lifted her head, meeting Lemon's gaze for the first time. She eked out a wry smile before her lips fell back into a frown. "No. My boss won't let me work the scene."

"Why not?" Mei asked.

Jade's eyes stayed on Lemon. "You remember that I told you I dated a cop for a while, about a year ago?"

It had been Jade's last serious relationship before they started up. And it hadn't ended well. "I remember."

Jade threw her thumb over her shoulder. "Berkeley Hyatt."

"Oh shit!" Mei's exclamation punctuated the space between them, even causing a stutter in Milo's snore.

"I've been helping search for her." Jade rubbed her left eye, the deep purple ring below became visible when she pulled her fingers away. "I've barely slept."

"I bet," Mei said. "That's messed up."

A tear fell down Jade's cheek. "And now she's dead."

Lemon had no words. She wished she knew what to say to comfort Jade. But her education in communications always failed her when emotions were involved.

"We're so sorry, Jade," Mei said.

Jade wiped at her cheek. "Did he find her?" Her gaze pinned on Milo.

"Yes," Lemon said.

Jade patted his back gently. "Good job, buddy. I hate to think of her out here alone. I'm glad you found her."

Silence blanketed the foursome. Even Milo's snoring stopped. The sounds from the crime scene drifted over on the light breeze, not quite distinguishable from the mumbling voices of the police or the gathered crowd of onlookers.

Bathed in a moment of peace, Lemon watched Jade stroke the apple-shaped light brown patch on Milo's back. Nothing changed what Milo found, what Mei's discovery led to, what Jade's former girlfriend had suffered. But in that moment, they had each other and a sense that nothing could pop their little bubble.

Until it did.

"Jade Milan." Detective Zahn's voice broke into their peace like a baseball thrown through a glass window.

Lemon glanced up at the detective and the two uniformed officers behind him.

"Detective. We meet again." Jade's voice, ice cold, echoed up as she rose to stand toe-to-toe with Zahn.

"I'm sorry, Ms. Milan. I know I've asked you a lot of questions lately."

"It's fine. I wanted Berkeley found."

"And so she is. And I have another question."

"Sure." Her expression remained hard. Her gaze shifted suddenly. Lemon followed it to see the red headed woman Jade identified as her boss jogging up to join the fray.

"Do you have your ID keycard for the lab with you?" Detective Zahn asked.

"Of course." Jade shoved her hand into the opening of her coveralls and produced a small, plastic card swinging from a dark, blue lanyard.

"Can you take it off, please?"

The look Jade shot the detective could fell large trees, but she yanked the lanyard off and handed it to him.

"Thank you." Zahn transferred the card to the red headed woman. Then he produced an identical one—complete with Jade's head shot in the right corner—wrapped in a plastic bag and handed it to the woman as well. "Tammy. Can you tell me which of these is the lab-issued ID card and which is the fake?"

The woman shuffled her gaze between the two cards for a moment before shoving her left hand forward, the plastic bag around the card crinkling loudly. "This one is real. The other is counterfeit."

Detective Zahn sighed. "That's what I was afraid of. Ms. Milan, do you have an explanation for why your badge was found near the body of Officer Hyatt?"

Lemon nearly threw up as she watched Jade's lips flutter before she pushed out. "What? What are you talking about?"

"Anything?" Zahn asked.

"No. Of course not!"

"All right then. Officer Plymouth. Please arrest Ms. Milan on the charge of murder."

Both uniformed officers enclosed Jade. Tears streamed down her face as one of them placed her in handcuffs and the other recited her Miranda rights.

Lemon shot to her feet, only to realize that Mei beat her to it. Milo stirred, his big nose pointed toward his guardian.

"Wait a minute. You can't arrest someone just like that," Mei said. "I watch true crime. That's not how it works!"

"This isn't all of a sudden, Ms. Lu." Zahn looked tired and sad, the lines around his eyes deep and dark. "Ms. Milan has been under suspicion since Officer Hyatt went missing."

"But this can't be all you have. A card. I mean. That is so circumstantial."

Zahn shook his head. "It's not all we have. Sorry ladies." He waved toward Milo, who'd managed to shuffle himself into a sitting position. "Thanks buddy."

Then he turned to follow the officers, between them a devastated Jade. Mei glanced at Lemon. "What the hell just happened?"

Chapter Three

Lemon stared at Mei. Mei stared back. The dogs—all three of them—kept their gazes pinned to the pizza on the counter.

"I can't believe it," Mei said for the third time.

Lemon scooped up a wedge of cheese pizza, examined it closely, then plopped it back down again. "They arrested Jade."

"For *murder*."

"I am…dumbfounded."

Mei chuckled. "I was going to say freaked out or fucked up or something a normal person would say, but yeah."

"What are we going to do?"

Mei gingerly bit off a tiny triangle of cheese, sauce, and bread, eyes turned up as she chewed. "The minute I saw those cuffs go on her I went into friend mode. I was like, okay we gotta get bail. But I'm pretty sure that's not so possible with murder charges."

"Yeah, I went through the same thing."

"Do we like, need to call her parents or something? A lawyer?"

Lemon's head snapped up. "What's wrong with me? Yeah, we should call her parents. Geez." She fumbled for her phone. It slid on the countertop, attempting to thwart her efforts. But she managed to grab it and punch up a contact.

"You have their phone number?"

"Remember that night I went out to their house in San Rafael for dinner and Jade drank vodka with her dad?"

"I feel like I remember that night, I guess."

"Well, they both passed out on the couch. Her mom insisted I have her cell number before I drove back across the bridge. So yeah, weirdly, I have her mom's number." Lemon hit the call button.

"Hello?" The voice echoed through the line, breathy and high-pitched, just as Lemon remembered it.

"Marla?"

"Yes?"

"It's Lemon. Lister. Lemon Lister."

"Oh, hi dear. Did you hear that Jade is in prison? Jade is in prison, sweetheart. I can't believe it! They actually arrested her and locked her up. They put her in prison!" The quick, frantic tone far exceeded her usually already excitable mode of speech.

"I think she's just down at the county jail right now," Mei said.

Mei didn't know what she was dealing with. In their evening together Lemon learned so many things about this woman. One of those things was that applying logic would get them nowhere.

"What? Who is that? Your new girlfriend? You moved on fast, didn't you?"

"No, that's my roommate." Lemon narrowed her eyes at Mei.

"What are you doing?" Marla asked.

"Um, what?"

"About Jade! What are you doing to get her out of prison?"

"What should I be doing?"

"We're on our way into the city now. That's what we're doing. We're headed to the prison to demand her release."

Mei leaned over the counter and whispered. "Is she going to the county jail or San Quentin, because I don't think she understands the difference between jail and prison?"

"Mei, shh," Lemon whispered back, stopping herself from jumping into the distraction to tell Mei that the California State prison for women was in Chino, not San Quentin. She focused instead on Jade's mother. "Do you think that's going to work?" Even as she asked Jade's mother the question, she flinched, expecting something truly bizarre in response.

A long pause greeted her question. Some mumbled conversation touched her ears. Perhaps Fred dropped reason on Marla during that interlude.

"Lemon?" Marla said.

"Yes?"

"Find out when the hearing is that determines the bail."

"Yeah, sure. I can try."

"You find out and call me back."

Lemon tangled her fingers together. "Okay. I will."

"Call me back."

The line went dead. Lemon glanced up at Mei. "I am so… I don't know."

"That woman is special."

"Yeah. She is. So, how do we find out about bail or whatever?"

"I got this." Mei pulled her own phone out of her pocket. "Leave it to me."

"How?"

Mei's finger flew across the phone. As the ringing sounded from the phone's speaker, she glanced up at Lemon with a smirk.

A voice came through the speaker. "Mei?"

"Hi Uncle Andy!"

"Sweet girl! How are you?"

"I'm in a bit of pickle, actually."

The deep voice on the other end of the line popped back. "Oh no! What's wrong?"

"A friend of mine just got arrested, and I have no idea how to help her."

"You need me to connect you to a bail bondsman?"

"Well, I'm not sure. I think maybe a lawyer is in order. A good one."

A deep, soothing chuckle carried through the phone line. "Well, I'm the best, but I only do serious crimes, sweetie. What is your friend accused of? Maybe I can connect them to someone?"

"Murder."

A beat of time passed before he spoke again. "Mei Lu, why do you know someone accused of murder?"

"She's a friend, and she didn't do it, Uncle."

"Does your mom know about this?"

Mei rolled her eyes. Lemon frowned at her. Whoever Uncle Andy was, he knew Mei's mom well. Lemon would almost prefer being accused of murder herself than deal with the freak-out that was bound to occur when Mrs. Lu found out about this.

"Not yet. Let's just keep it on the down low for now."

"Good luck with that kid. Okay, what's your friend's name, and who arrested her? SFPD?"

"Yes. Her name is Jade Milan. She works at the crime lab. Detective Zahn arrested her a few hours ago."

Uncle Andy whistled. "Detective Zahn doesn't arrest innocent people, sweetie. This could be a tough one. Also, did your friend already ask for a lawyer? Maybe she's got a public defender down there now? Or maybe someone else."

"I don't know, Uncle. But she needs *you*."

"Okay. I'll check it out. Standby, kiddo. I'll call you later."

"Thanks Uncle Andy. I love you."

"Love you, too, kid. Bye."

Lemon reached across the counter and grabbed Mei's wrist. "Who the hell is Uncle Andy, and why haven't I ever met him?"

"He's Aunt Sue's third husband."

"I thought Tommy was her third husband."

"No, Tommy is her second husband."

"So your Uncle Hector is her fourth husband?"

"No, Hector is her fifth. Bobby is her fourth."

"Damn. I'm confused."

"Aunt Sue loves men."

"Okay wait. I have met pretty much all of Sue's exes at family dinners. Why haven't I met your Uncle Andy?"

"He's been living in San Diego for the last ten years. He just moved back to San Francisco. He used to be a prosecutor in SF before he switched sides to become a defense attorney. He knows *everybody* in the city. He followed a woman down south. They divorced, and he's back. Semi-retired. But I knew I could count on his help. He loves me."

"Of course he does." Lemon knew that being the only girl in her generation made Mei the focus of a lot of doting and love by her massive family. It figured some long lost uncle would drop everything to help her out. "So what do we do now?"

Mei picked up the remains of her pizza slice. "We wait for Uncle Andy to call us back."

Lemon stared down at her own meal, any potential for an appetite fled as she pictured her sort-of-girlfriend lying on a hard cot shoved into the corner of a cold, concrete and steel jail cell accused of the absolute worst crime.

****

The barking started a half-second after the first pulse of the knock on their door. All three dogs—gathered in a semi-circle around her on the bed, with Klee and Snickers on either side of her legs and Milo sprawled out at her feet—protested loudly to the nighttime bandit they heard attempting to disturb their peaceful night's sleep.

Ears ringing, Lemon leapt up and shimmied into a pair of yoga pants. All three pups beat her to the bedroom door, bolting out as soon as she pulled it open. Klee and Snickers led the way with Milo waddling along behind them. Mei nearly tripped on his long body as she emerged from her own room, her straight black hair swinging wildly as she shoved her arms into a zip-up hoodie.

"Coming!"

Just behind Mei, Lemon kept pace, rubbing her eyes. Sleep had never come, but exhaustion arrived early. That tended to happen when her brain whirled in ever increasing circles.

Snickers ran around Mei's ankles as she lined up her right eye with the peephole. Without announcing what she saw on the other side of the door, Mei leaned back and swung it open.

Snickers plunged into the interior apartment hallway to conduct a close-up inspection of the visitor, while Milo and Klee waited for him to step across the threshold. Tall, tan, muscular, and impossibly blond, a man who could easily pass for a retired professional surfer greeted Mei with a hug.

When Mei emerged from his embrace, she turned to Lemon. "Uncle Andy, this is my bestie, Lemon."

"Ah, yes. Lemon Lister, the dog walker." He held out his hand. Lemon noticed a cute dimple pinned to one of his cheeks as he smiled at her. "Nice to meet you."

Lemon shook his hand and backed out of the small entryway to allow him space to get in the door. She coaxed Snickers back in and toward him so Mei could close them all into the apartment. Andy stripped off his light jacket. Lemon instinctively reached out to take it, placing it over a barstool as they passed the kitchen on their way to the living room.

"You need a drink?" Mei asked.

Andy dropped into the loveseat. "No thanks. I know it's late. I won't stay long. I just wanted to fill you in."

Mei settled beside him. Lemon plopped into the couch opposite them and accepted Snickers in her lap. Klee snuggled up beside her thigh, and Milo threw himself over her feet. "Thanks for coming by."

"I know you're worried. I wanted to let you know I was able to meet with Jade. She did ask for a lawyer pretty much as soon as she was arrested. They stuck her back in a cell until she could be appointed a public defender. But she won't need that anymore."

"So you took her case?" Mei clasped his hand in her own.

"Yes, sweetie, I did. But I have to tell you, it doesn't look good."

"Why not?" Lemon asked.

Andy turned his attention to her, his blue eyes sincere. "Well, there is a lot of circumstantial evidence against your friend. But she says she's innocent. And I believe her. If you do?"

"Yes." Lemon was certain Jade could never hurt anyone.

"Of course we do," Mei said. "There's no way she did this."

Andy's kind smile radiated through the room. "Okay then. I'll do my best."

Mei skipped over his generous offer to ask another favor. "Are you gonna tell us about what they have?"

Lemon wanted to inject herself into the conversation to thank Andy first and foremost, but she was too slow on the uptake. Andy rushed into the explanation. "Here's what I know so far: Jade was on the list of suspects as soon as Berkeley went missing."

"Wait. Why?" Mei asked.

"She's the most recent significant other. That's always the first go to, current or most immediate past girlfriend."

"But they broke up almost a year ago." Lemon's chest tightened, hoping what Jade told her was true.

"Yes. But according to Detective Zahn, Berkeley hasn't dated since."

"Okay, so Jade's the automatic suspect. But that doesn't mean she actually did it," Mei said.

One side of Andy's mouth curled up. "It absolutely doesn't. And, sweetie, I am the king of defending significant others."

One of the taut strings running through Lemon's nervous system relaxed, sagging with relief. At least something went right. On the long list of things to do accumulating in her brain, she crossed off finding a good lawyer. If Andy's confidence and swagger was earned, Jade might be in good hands.

"So what else do they have?" Mei asked.

"I can tell you what I found out during the interview."

"You sat for an interview, voluntarily?" Mei asked.

"That's why I'm so late. I wanted to know what they had, and it was the fastest way to find out. So, yeah, we sat with Detective Zahn and his partner and let them show their hand."

"Surely Detective Zahn is too smart for that." Lemon probably didn't need to point this out. Andy must know Detective Zahn was no spring chicken.

"Oh sure. But he did it anyway. Which is odd. He sat there, with a green detective at his side and asked me a bunch of telling questions, while I told Jade not to answer them. It was—to put it mildly—a rookie mistake. Which makes me wonder…"

Lemon's chest tightened. "Wonder what?"

"I don't want to speculate. Let me just tell you what I absolutely know."

"Please," Mei said.

Andy crossed one leg over the other, bouncing his foot, the light brown leather of his shoe catching Lemon's eye. "Jade and Berkeley spoke on the phone seven times during the three days leading up to her disappearance."

"Did Jade say why?" Mei asked.

"No. I told her not to. She didn't answer any of these questions. I will find out the answers to them myself later. For now, what's important is what the police know."

Mei's expression reflected that of a student listening to a wizened professor. "Okay."

"They asked about the last time Jade was in Berkeley's car. We didn't answer. And they pushed, asking why a sweatshirt of Jade's was found in the trunk of Berkeley's car. So they have that. And they have proof it was Jade's. Co-workers had seen Jade wearing that sweatshirt within a few days of Berkeley's disappearance."

"Okay. So they saw each other," Mei said.

"No. Not according to Jade."

Lemon's muddled mind needed answers. "Wait, I thought you didn't ask her these questions?"

"I didn't, but she willingly participated in two interviews during the time Berkeley was missing. And they followed up on things she said during those interviews. Apparently, she said she hadn't seen Berkeley, outside of a few run-ins at work, in over nine months. So, the police wanted to know how her clothing ended up in Berkeley's car."

"But you didn't let her answer, did you?" Mei asked.

"Of course not."

"Still seems a little light for murder charges," Lemon said.

"It is. Even when you add in the insurance policy."

"Insurance policy?" Mei asked.

"Yeah. Jade was listed as the second beneficiary after Berkeley's mother."

Mei let out a pfft of air. "Second isn't very strong,"

"It is when Berkeley's mom died three weeks ago."

"Damn. That doesn't look good," Mei said.

"No, sweetie. It does not. Then there was the kicker."

"Which was?" Lemon' fingers plunged into Snickers fur as she prepared herself for the blow.

Andy's tone was flat and hard. "They found her work ID with the body."

"We know. We were there. Milo." Mei pointed to the sleeping hound, piled on top of Lemon's feet. "He found the body."

Andy's gaze drifted from Mei to Lemon and back again. "They say she had a counterfeit ID on her person, and the real one was with the body."

"Yeah. Her supervisor basically glanced at them both and declared the one that was with the stiff to be the real one," Mei said.

"Interesting. Well, that's the physical evidence they put together with the circumstantial evidence to charge her."

"So what do we do now?" Lemon asked.

"I'm going to try to get bail. Then we fight." Andy grinned. "I forgot how exhilarating a murder trial is. I don't know why I wanted to retire."

Mei gave her uncle a soft punch to his arm. "See, uncle, I got you covered."

The levity didn't touch Lemon's stressed out brain.

Chapter Four

Lemon's lungs burned as she skipped up the concrete steps of the courthouse. Mei's breath echoed hard and ragged behind her. They burst into the courthouse lobby and nearly ran headlong into a security guard.

He spoke in a low, bored tone. "Please place your belongs in a bin and run it through the metal detector."

Mei held up her arms, demonstrating that neither she nor Lemon carried a purse or bag. "We literally don't have anything."

The security guard raised one eyebrow. "Really? You mean to tell me you don't have a phone or set of keys hiding in your pockets?"

"Yes. We do. Thank you," Lemon said politely. She shoved her hand in her pocket and retrieved both her phone and her massive set of keys. The security guard raised an eyebrow, probably questioning why Lemon's "I heart dogs" key ring was attached to at least a dozen house keys, all color coded.

Mei threw her own phone and keys into a brown plastic bucket. She pivoted on her heel and marched through the metal detector, smirking back at Lemon when the machine remained silent.

Lemon followed her through with the same result. They collected their belongings before jogging toward the elevator. After an excruciating wait that had Lemon wondering why they didn't just take the stairs, the car arrived. A gaggle of people poured out of the elevator, including Mei's Uncle Andy and Jade's parents.

"You missed it," Andy said. He placed a hand on Mei's upper back and led her to an alcove off the lobby. "The hearing just finished."

Marla and Fred Milan crowded around Andy and Mei. Lemon hovered on the edge, an uncomfortable sensation crawling up her spine.

"I refuse to accept this!" Marla said, her voice loud and screechy.

Andy must be used to people like Marla Milan. While he reacted without a single flinch, Lemon fought the deep desire to hide in a closet until Jade's mother was safely north of the Golden Gate Bridge.

Mei's uncle spoke gently. "I understand completely. But given the circumstances, the judge had no other choice. He couldn't give her bail. She's a flight risk."

"She didn't get bail?" Lemon asked.

"Afraid not."

"What circumstances? How is she a flight risk?" Mei's arms flailed around, nearly striking a regal statue on the nose.

Lemon gulped in air as Andy turned his gaze on her. "The plane tickets you and she have."

"What?" Lemon swayed on her feet, the marble floor of the courthouse a very real threat to her safety.

"They found an electronic trail. Two plane tickets—one in your name, and one in Jade's—leaving for Mexico tomorrow."

"What?" Lemon's thoughts swam in a murk thicker than the San Francisco fog.

Andy cocked his head. "You didn't know?"

"No. No. Absolutely not. Are you sure one of the tickets was in my name?"

"I saw the tickets," Andy said.

Lemon gaped. None of this made any sense.

"That's way weird," Mei said. "Way weird."

"Agreed." Andy said. "Very strange."

Marla had her own point to make. "Jade would have told us if she was leaving town."

"I'm sure," Andy said.

"Maybe whoever is framing Jade for the murder bought the tickets," Mei said.

"Good thought." Andy clapped his hands together. "I know someone I can put on that. Follow the electronic trail."

"Do it!" Marla demanded. "Find out who's framing my daughter."

Andy placed a hand on Marla's shoulder. "Absolutely, Ms. Milan. I'm all over it."

Lemon felt the urge to remind everyone that Andy was working for free, and probably shouldn't be bossed around like a plebian. "Thank you, Andy. I know this is a big case to take on pro bono."

The grin he shot her was so charming Lemon had a split second of attraction to the man twice her age and three times her status and power. "It's my pleasure."

"What about bail?" Marla asked. "Can we still get that?"

Andy pointed to the courtroom they just left, his patience appearing to Lemon to be saint-like. "There's no changing that, ma'am. The judge ruled that she be held over until trial. So I'm afraid she'll be in jail until then."

Marla gripped Andy's shoulder, her knuckles turning pale under the harsh florescent lights. "That could take months!"

"At the very least, yes," Andy said.

Marla attempted to shake Andy, but his large frame didn't move. Only the soft fabric of his jacket shifted in response. "This is unacceptable!"

"I agree. I wish I could do something," Andy said.

Marla Milan appeared to be contemplating some act that may or may not land her in jail with her daughter when Fred reached out and hooked his arm around his wife's waist. "We appreciate your help Andy."

Marla's hands fell her to sides. But Andy didn't take a step back to get away from her, instead he reached out to Fred for a handshake. "I still have a lot of work to do. Thank me when she gets off."

With a few muttered goodbyes, the Milans headed off toward the courthouse entrance, leaving a deep silence in their wake until Mei broke it. "Uncle Andy, can we buy you lunch?"

"Tell you what, why don't you two let me buy you lunch. I'm quite certain there is a lot more in my bank account." He placed a hand on each of their elbows, leading them back into the main lobby. "How does Thai sound?"

****

Lemon swirled her chopsticks through sinewy rice noodles. "So there's really nothing we can do to get Jade out of jail?"

"I don't know. If I can prove those tickets are fake, maybe, *maybe*, I can file a motion. Chances are not good, though. I'm sorry."

"So, what did Jade tell you about all this? I mean, did you get to talk to her?" Mei asked.

With a robust bite of Penang Curry in his mouth, Andy nodded.

"But you can't tell us, right?" Lemon said. "Attorney, client privilege and all that?"

Andy swallowed hard. "On the contrary. She gave me permission to talk with you two, and I'm planning to employ you."

"Employ us?" Mei asked.

Andy chuckled. "Perhaps I misspoke. Since I'm working for free, I expect you to as well. Perhaps volunteer is the right word."

"What can we do?" Lemon asked. Despite squeaking by each month on her bills, pay landed on the bottom of her list of cares at the moment. If she could help Jade, she would.

Andy abandoned his fork, leaving it to hang precariously half off his plate. "I'm glad you asked. I need researchers. And the ones I usually hire, they don't work for free. The Milans don't have much money to spend on this trial, and Jade's cash is tied up in her business, so I need help."

"Wait. Back up," Mei said. "Her *business*? She works at the crime lab."

"And she has a business," Andy casually took a sip of his drink. Lemon didn't know what exactly was in his glass since, she didn't understand his order when he made it, but it was something alcoholic with ice cubes swimming in light brown liquid.

Mei turned to Lemon, her mouth agape. "Did you know about this?"

Resisting the urge to remind Mei that she explained Jade's side business to her early on but Mei either paid no attention or forgot, Lemon simply said, "Yes."

Andy took another sip, his bright eyes gazing at Lemon over the rim of the glass. "Have you ever met her business partner?"

"Yeah." A knot formed in Lemon's gut, pulling at her insides uncomfortably.

"I have a meeting with him tomorrow. What are your thoughts?"

Lemon bit her lip. How much should she say? Her fear of creating a suspicion where it may not exist warred with her desire to help until she finally decided that only the truth would do in this situation. "I never got a good feeling about him. But I can't really explain why. It wasn't like it was anything Tony ever did. It was just a feeling, you know? I mean, also, I only met him a few times. I could be wrong."

Mei said, "Lemon has good instincts. But I need a little catch up here. Can someone please tell me what the hell is going on? What is this side hustle Jade has with this sketchy partner?"

"Crime scene cleanup," Andy said. "She and a former cop named Tony Jillian are in it together. Fifty-fifty. And he claims all the money is tied up in the business. Not a dime available to help Jade." He pressed his lips together. "I don't like it. It's not right."

Lemon was unsure how to articulate why that didn't come as a surprise to her. Something about Tony rubbed her the wrong way from the moment Lemon first met him at Jade's birthday dinner. She wished Mei had been there that night as well. She welcomed a second opinion.

"So, this partner, would he have a reason to kill Berkeley?" Mei asked.

"I have no idea," Andy said.

"But you'll ask him, right?"

"I might need to be a bit more subtle. Leave the interviewing to me. I have a different job for the two of you."

"What can we do?" Lemon asked.

Andy rested his elbows on the table and leaned forward. A skiff of stubble on his chin glowed in the sunlight. Lemon involuntarily curved her lips upward. Attraction always created that reaction in her.

"I have a basic sketch of Jade's connections. I need you to expand that for me, like a web."

"Or a game of Six Degrees of Kevin Bacon," Mei suggested.

"Sure. Like that. I give you a name, and you find out all the people they know. And we go from there."

"So we *will* be interviewing people." Lemon thought the enthusiasm clear in Mei's voice was completely uncalled for.

"No. Not interviewing. Much subtler than that." Andy rapped his fingers on the table. "Who am I talking to? You, my sweet niece, do not excel in subtle."

Mei shoved her thumb toward Lemon. "Maybe not. But *she* does."

"Hmm," Andy rubbed his chin. "I had planned to give you separate assignments. But perhaps you should work as a team."

Lemon glanced over at Mei. Best friends absolutely. Partners in crime. Sure. A team for a delicate job. Meh. Perhaps not. "I don't know. I mean, we interact with people so very differently…"

"It's perfect. We're a great team. We solved *two* murders last year."

"Milo solved two murders last year," Lemon said. "And we had help from Jade." Another wave of fear rolled over her as she realized

Jade sat in jail at that very moment.

Mei rolled her eyes and leaned toward her uncle. "We got this. Who's first?"

Andy glanced at his phone, scrolling slowly with his finger, teeth biting into his lower lip. "I want you to wait on Tony until after *I* talk to him. So I think you should start with Felicia Kelly. Do you know her?"

Lemon's gaze pinned on Mei. Were they thinking the same thing?

"Yeah. We know her. She's in our book club. Why is she on the list?"

"A week ago Jade filed a restraining order against her," Andy said.

Shock overrode everything, making Lemon jolt in her seat. "What? Why?"

"Jade said Felicia has been asking her out regularly for a couple months and not taking no for an answer. Then when she found out you and Jade weren't together anymore." Andy pointed his finger at Lemon. "She got aggressive about it, and Jade got the restraining order. I need you two to find out what you can, and find out what connections Felicia has. I'm doubtful Felicia will talk, but maybe we can find someone who knows something who will. Understand?"

"Perfectly," Lemon said. "We're on it."

Chapter Five

Lemon always associated Hayley's cozy living room with books and wine. Of course she was the president and founder of their Sapphic book club, so the association was completely logical. But it might be better characterized as a set from an Agatha Christie novel, because it seemed they were always sitting on the overstuffed furniture trying to solve a murder.

"Poor Jade," Hayley said. "I can't believe this, first her ex goes missing and she's totally freaked out, spends all this time searching. I mean she worked her regular shift at the lab every day then went out and searched all evening. She looked exhausted the last time I saw her. And now she's in jail. I mean, holy hell!"

"It's definitely a shock," Lemon said. "We're working with her lawyer to help gather any information we can to help her out."

"I'm in." Hayley tilted forward. "How can I help?"

Lemon shifted to face Mei, fully chickening out on making the big ask.

Mei understood the assignment. "What do you know about Felicia?"

"Oh," Hayley placed her mug carefully on the coffee table and sat back. "Yeah. That's a bit of a mess."

Blood sped through Lemon's veins. The truth felt close. Could it be this easy? "So you know what happened between Jade and Felicia?"

"Not everything. I mean, I probably know more than most people because one of my best friends is Hayley's bff since they were in school."

"Tell us everything you know." Mei rubbed her hands together like an evil scientist.

"Well, the story I've heard from other people is probably what you heard." Hayley tipped her head at Lemon. "Felicia's had a thing for Jade since they met. She backed off when you and Jade started dating. But then she heard you guys were on a break or whatever, she came on hard. Jade filed a restraining order after Felicia followed her one night from one bar to the next when she was out with her work friends. They kept bar hopping to get away from her, but she ended up at each new place. It creeped Jade out."

"I'd be creeped out, too" Mei said.

Felicia cringed. "Yeah. It doesn't make Felicia look very good. For sure. But it's not the real story. Miles says there's a lot more to it."

"Her best friend?"

"Yeah, he told me that Felicia did come on strong but that she was in a cult, and it was part of their advice."

Lemon's jaw was still in free-fall when Mei shouted. "What? Wait. What?"

"There's a podcast about it. Check it out. It's totally true. This couple had an online cult where they convinced their followers to basically stalk and harass their crushes, who they claimed were their soul mates and they were destined to be together. You can't make this shit up."

"That is…wow," Mei said.

"I think I read about that," Lemon said. "There were all kinds of people who ended up in jail or with restraining orders because these gurus were pushing them to do all this super stalky shit."

"Yeah, so that's the first part. And she's out of the cult now and admits that she crossed the line. But the restraining order, that's not what everyone says it is. Miles didn't give me details. It was a quick conversation, and we both had to go."

"We really need to know about that," Lemon said, her assignment heavy on her mind. "Is there any way you can find out what happened?"

Hayley tapped her finger against her chin. "I guess I could ask him." She stopped tapping and bounced in her seat. "Or better yet, you could. How about I arrange for us to meet up for a drink. How does that sound?"

Mei grinned. "That sounds perfect."

****

Lemon's knee bounced under the table. Mei reached over and slammed her palm down on it for the second time. Her knee and her nerves seemed to be out of control from the moment they arrived at the restaurant to meet up with Marla and Fred Milan.

Marla's constant speech, which increased in pitch and anxiety every few minutes, wasn't helping. Though neither Fred nor Mei seemed affected. Both sat, opposite one another, backs sunk into the curved wooden booth, arms tucked somewhere beneath the thick oak table between them.

Lemon, on the other hand, stared across at Marla, her hands and mouth in constant motion, red-rimmed eyes wide and moving so quickly that motion-sickness began to rise in Lemon's stomach.

"Andy says she's perfectly safe in there, but how can that be? She helped put some of those people away! How is that safe?"

Fred grabbed hold of one of Marla's flailing hands and gently dropped it to the table, keeping it pinned beneath his own. "None of those people have a clue who she is, sweetheart. She works behind the scenes in the lab, doesn't have anything to do with the interviews or interrogations, and she very rarely testifies in court. She's too far down on the ladder for them to be concerned with her."

Rather than providing comfort, his reassurance seemed to twist some unseen knife in Marla's back. She ripped her hand out from beneath his and jammed her newly freed finger into his chest. "Her work is important! She puts away bad guys!"

With the entirety of the small bistro staring at them, Lemon shrunk into the curved wood at her back just as Mei straightened up, leaned forward, and took charge.

"Mrs. Milan. Marla."

Marla's head snapped up, her glare focused on Mei. "What?"

"We need to get to work." Mei took a deep breath, as if she were trying to demonstrate calm to the frantic woman. "We have work to do. How about if you let Lemon and I ask you some questions? So we can help Andy help Jade. That's what we all want, right?"

Whether or not Marla appreciated being spoken to as if she were a petulant child in need of redirection—and Lemon was pretty sure she did not—there was little argument to be made in the face of such logic. Marla lowered her attacking arm, placing it on her lap. She straightened her spine, let her lips relax and held her gaze on Mei.

Mei took the unspoken communication as agreement and plunged on. "We need to know everything you know about Felicia."

"Felicia?" Fred asked.

"Yeah. That's the woman who was stalking Jade."

"Stalking her?" Marla leaned forward, her ribs hitting the side of the table, her breasts brushing the surface.

"Um, I take it you didn't know about this?" Mei asked.

"No, we didn't. Who is this person?" Fred asked.

"We don't know much yet. But we're working on it. Right now, we're just filing her into a drawer of people we need to know more about, okay?"

Mei's tidy wrap-up of the Felicia-situation did not have an equally tidy response from the Milans. Both still had furrowed brows and squinted eyes. Almost identical expressions of confusion and surprise reflected back at Lemon and Mei from across the clean wooden surface, littered with coffee cups and napkins.

Mei shifted the conversation. "Let's talk about someone else, Tony, Jade's business partner. What can you tell us about him?"

Fred looked as if he might protest the change in subject, but whatever he was about to say was interrupted by the server. No matter how many times she saw someone do it, Lemon could never understand how they balanced four plates in two arms and then managed to slide them into place on the table without creating a cataclysmic disaster.

Lemon ran her finger over the same few inches of cream-colored porcelain at the edge of her plate as she waited for the conversation to resume. But the intense pause drew out like a long stretch of melted cheese on a piece of pizza, clinging to its origin as it gets farther away.

Marla stabbed her fork into the omelet in front of her, but did not break the silent stand-down. As soon as his Eggs Benedict arrived, Fred shoved a heaping forkful into his mouth.

The Milans couldn't have fully understood the choice they were making when they allowed Mei to determine the course of the rest of the conversation. They may as well have waved a white flag.

"So, Tony, the business partner. We don't know a thing about this guy except that he's an ex-cop. I mean, have you met him?" Mei asked.

Marla, looking like an assassin with her eyes squinted and her fork still jutting out of the robust omelette, didn't move to answer. Fred, however, nodded even as he continued to chew.

Whether it was Fred's nod or something else that struck Marla with the sudden urge to move past their previous argument and move forward into their relationship, Lemon wasn't sure. But Marla definitely signaled that intent. Her eyes opened wide, her shoulders softened and she spoke, her voice calm and quiet—or at least relative to any other moment Lemon had spent with her.

"We liked him, all right. Came around with Jade and pitched the business to us. We invested, so did his brother."

"Good investment," Fred said. "We already got half of what we gave them back. The business was doing good. They had more work than the two of them—especially with Jade still working full-time—could even handle. They turned away a few jobs."

"So you trust him?" Mei asked.

"I don't know about that," Fred said.

Mei leaned forward, nearly plowing into her stack of pancakes. "Really? Why's that?"

"He seems to have a good head on his shoulders, he seems to be good with money, and his family supports him. Ex-cop. Ex-military. I mean, what's not to trust?" Fred said.

"But you're the one who said you didn't really trust him."

"I'll tell you why we don't trust him," Marla said, bringing the unfolding argument to an abrupt stop. "Because he has a temper."

Lemon couldn't help the tone that leapt from her tightened throat. "Like he hit Jade?"

"No. Not that we know of," Fred said. "But we've heard him lose it. He's a real screamer that one. Says the nastiest things. Last time we were at her apartment he came over and threw a tantrum, I kicked him out."

Marla scoffed. When the attention of everyone at the table turned to her, she smirked. "*I* threw him out."

Fred shrugged. "Anyway, he was being an ass."

"When was this?" Lemon asked, her brain pulling up a visual calendar.

Fred and Marla exchanged a glance, as if they were forcing the answer through a pooled set of thoughts. "Maybe two weeks ago," Marla said.

"Sounds right," Fred said.

"So this big fight was two weeks ago?" Mei asked.

As Fred and Marla both affirmed that statement, Lemon jumped in. "What did they fight about?"

"The same as always, time."

"Time? What do you mean?" Lemon asked.

"Tony is retired, or so he says. A bit on the young side for someone not invested in big tech if you ask me. But then again maybe he is." Fred shrugged. "The guy is smart. Anyway, he worked full-time on the business. But Jade works at the lab a lot. And she's been pulling double-shifts and doing extra work a lot for the last couple months. That leaves Tony all alone. And what they do is a hard. And gross, and, well it's a lot of work."

Lemon had no desire to picture the heinous scenes that confronted Jade daily in either of her jobs. One encounter with a severed foot and the more recent invasion of her nostrils with ode de corpse were enough for a lifetime. And that—that was ultimately why she sat across from Jade's parents as the presumptive ex-girlfriend at this very moment.

Lemon cleared her throat. "She was working a lot more. She said it was because Tammy had scared everyone else off."

Fred pointed his finger at Lemon. "That's true. That's what happened with Tony. He was actually working with Tammy when he up and quit the force. By then he and Jade met and devised the business scheme. They'd even already gotten some investments. So it wasn't terrible timing."

"But," Marla grabbed Fred's finger, shoving it down so she could stare over at Lemon unencumbered. "From that day on he bugged her to quit, too."

"Jade's too smart for that. She's fifteen years younger than Tony. She can't afford to give up a steady paycheck and health insurance for a gamble on a business that might not pan out."

"So they argued about this?" Mei asked.

"All the time," Marla said.

"I hate to ask," Lemon said, "but why didn't he just get another partner? Or hire someone?"

"Because they were already intertwined money-wise. Half and half. They owed family and friends who put money in. And they couldn't afford to hire someone, not yet at least."

Realization hit Lemon like a truck. "So he meant it when he said all the money was tied up in the business and he couldn't get bail for Jade?"

"I believe that's true," Fred said.

"Not that it matters." Marla leaned in. "That goddam judge wouldn't give her bail anyway."

"But wait!" Mei threw her hand into the air above the table as if she were anxious to be called on by the teacher, her hand nearly crashed into Marla's nose. "If the money is tied up in the business and what he really needs is her help, he has no motive to put her behind bars."

"Not necessarily," Fred said. "They have right of survivorship on the business. With her out of the way, he gets all of it, even the investment money she brought in."

"But she's not dead. She's in jail," Mei said. "If he wanted the business it would make way more sense to kill Jade than to frame her for murder…Sorry."

"She's right though," Lemon said. "It doesn't make sense."

"Well, if it's not him, then who?" Marla's voice cracked on the last word. She cleared her throat and repeated the question. "Who?"

"I don't know," Lemon said. But she wished she did.

Chapter Six

Some mornings three dogs felt like too many. All hell broke loose nearly as soon as they got back from breakfast with the Milans. Snickers didn't want to eat the special food the vet prescribed him to keep his skin from getting itchy. Klee, after battling Snickers for his own, apparently much tastier food, decided to hide under Mei's bed and refuse to come out for any reason what-so-ever. And Milo, determined that the delivery person was trying to rob the house, bayed non-stop until they were out of sight.

"Can I please drop them off at the shelter today?" Mei asked casually as she dropped her lunch into her backpack. "I will take them on my way to work. You don't have to do it."

"Stop." Lemon turned to the dogs, all three of whom were now lying at her feet with big, sad eyes pointed directly at her. "She's just kidding guys."

"No, she's not," Mei said.

"You have time for a latte?" Lemon shook a mug at Mei. It didn't matter how much coffee they'd had at the restaurant, they would both need more.

"Yeah, I told my boss I'd be in late, so I can get there whenever." Mei slumped down in the barstool beside Lemon. "Don't you have dogs to walk though?"

Lemon turned toward the fancy espresso machine Mei's parents had gifted to them and started prepping their drinks. "I got Kimberly to take the morning crew today. I knew we'd be too late getting back from breakfast. And also Andy said he would call."

Mei glanced at her phone. "Ugh. My date might have to cancel tonight."

"I didn't know you had a date. Who is it? That girl from the gym?"

"No. Caroline."

"Caroline? Who's Caroline?"

Mei huffed a sigh. "Really? The super hot K-9 cop at the park. Don't tell me you didn't notice her?"

Lemon noticed how snotty she was, and how much she dissed on

Milo's abilities without knowing anything about him, like that he solved two murders with his awesome nose or that he is obsessed with finding dead things. "Um, yeah."

"Yeah, so. I got her number, and we've been texting."

"Well that's weird."

"Why? What's weird about it?"

"Let's see. You met at crime scene. And we found a dead body. And it was also the day your friend got arrested. So…yeah…tough story to tell the grandkids."

"Fate is fate, my friend. Don't be a jealous bitch."

Lemon shook her head, attempting to work up a good comeback, but she was interrupted by the ringing phone.

Mei hit a button on the screen. "Uncle Andy."

"Hi sweetie. How are you?"

"Tired. How about you?"

Andy chuckled. "You youngins sleep too much. I've been up for a bit working on your friend's case."

"Oh yeah. We got up early and spent an hour with Marla Milan. Top that."

Before they could get into a back and forth about which fate was worse, Lemon leaned toward the phone and yelled into the speaker. "What you got?"

"I interviewed Tony Jillian, and I just finished some last minute research on him before I called. I can't pin anything on the guy, but he was acting weird the whole conversation."

"Weird how?" Lemon asked.

"I can't describe it. But trust me on this. I've met a lot of weird dudes. And this guy wasn't a ten on the spooky scale, but he was a solid seven."

"Marla and Fred said he and Jade fought over her working her other job too much. He wanted her to quit to help make the business a success," Mei said.

"Wait. I thought she met him at the crime lab. Didn't he work there, too?"

"He quit. Apparently there was something that went down between him and their boss Tammy."

"Tammy Ryder? Head of the lab?"

"Yes. Tammy," Lemon said. "You know her?"

"Only because of this case. She doesn't go back to my time. But Tony didn't tell me any of this. Listen, look into Tammy. That's your next assignment. Gotta go. Talk to you soon."

Lemon glanced up a Mei. "How the hell do we investigate a complete stranger?"

"We'll think of something."

****

Lemon sucked at bars. The ultimate wallflower, she shut down completely in them. Her social anxiety always seemed to find new avenues to explore when confronted with a tightly packed room of drunken women. Though this time the dynamic shifted a bit. Aside from Hayley, Lemon, Mei, and a conspicuous group from a bachelorette party, everyone crammed into the tiny, brick building were men.

Miles slammed into the chair beside Hayley. "Ladies, this place is lit!"

"Here drink this," Hayley handed him a tall pint of beer.

He took a long gulp as if beer could somehow quench his thirst after a rambunctious bout of dancing. He dropped the pint to the table and licked the foam off his upper lip. "Sorry. You wanted to talk?"

"We want to know about Felicia and Jade. It's important," Hayley said.

Miles took another long sip, dropping the level of beer in his glass to just under half. He slammed it down and let out a heavy breath. "Okay. Let's do this. I talked to Felicia, and she said I could tell you everything. She wants to help Jade, but she knows she's a bit of a persona non grata lately. So here I am." He opened his arms wide, showing off his tight blue shirt. "Where do you want me to start?"

"At the beginning," Mei said.

"Okay. Yeah. Felilcia had a thing for Jade. She came on strong. And Jade said she was working on a thing with you." Miles gestured with his head toward Lemon. "So she backed off. At first. But then she enrolled in this freaking class. The whole thing was about finding your other half, your soul mate. I'm not really sure what made her sign up. It's not like it was ever a big deal before. But one night she went out with this friend of hers, Jemma." Miles rolled his eyes. "And the next day she was signed up for this soul mate class. And then all of a sudden she's convinced that Jade is the one person on this planet she's supposed to be with. And the culty gurus who run this class convinced her that she had to fight for Jade."

Lemon's stomach churned. The issue that led to the temporary break with Jade was something she'd hoped they would overcome. She hadn't given up on them. And now, in the middle of all this chaos she was hearing that someone else wanted her girlfriend? She swallowed hard. "So, what did Felicia do?"

Miles rubbed his cheek. "It started pretty innocent, really. She would call, send cards, flowers, that kind of thing. Jade was very straight forward with Felicia. She told her flat out she wasn't interested. I mean, she wasn't mean, at least not in my opinion. But she was super clear, leaving no room for miscommunication. But when Felicia told these scammers about it, they told her to double down, to chase her soul mate. So she got more aggressive. Calling and texting and more flowers. I swear, I tried to reason with her, but between the culty fucks and this Jemma person, she was completely lost, caught up in stalking Jade in the name of true love. It was fucked up."

"What about the restraining order?" Lemon asked.

"Getting there. First, you have to know that it all ended about two weeks before that incident. Someone else in the group got arrested for stalking, and Felicia just woke up." Miles snapped his fingers. "She apologized to Jade via text and never called her or bothered her again."

"Until that night at the bars," Mei said. "Right?"

"Yeah." Miles sighed and folded his arms over his chest. "That night. That's a whole other story."

Lemon leaned over the table, something sticky catching on her wrist. "What's the story?"

"She was trying to warn Jade that night."

Lemon's heartbeat sped up, the thumping providing a chilling backdrop to her rising anxiety. "Warn her? Warn her about what?"

"Some guy named Gaylen was looking for Jade. He contacted Felicia and was desperate to get in touch with Jade. Felicia thought the whole thing was super creepy. She tried to leave messages for Jade, but she was blocked. So that night when she saw her at the bar, she tried to talk to her. But Jade and her friends wouldn't have it. They kept running from Felicia, and she kept following Jade." Miles ran a hand over his forehead. "I love that girl, but what a dumbass. I asked her why the hell didn't she just get me to call Jade? Jesus. Anyway, she ended up arrested. What a fucking mess."

Lemon's stomach flipped over. "She was trying to warn her?"

"Yeah. And after she ended up in jail, I bailed her out and took her on a vacay to San Diego where my folks live. Girl needed some down time. That's where we were from before Berkeley went missing until yesterday. So she has an alibi, too. I'm telling you, my girl is stupid, but totally innocent."

Stiff and wooden, Lemon's body reflected the whirlwind of conflicting thoughts streaming through her brain. Felicia and Jade's situation was complex. Jade kept it all from Lemon. Felicia claimed some creeper was looking for Jade. Felicia couldn't have killed Berkeley. It all merged together into a muddy river of facts and feelings.

"We appreciate your help," Mei said.

"I appreciate you making sure my friend's name doesn't get dragged into this mess," Miles said.

"We're on it," Mei said. "We're only after the truth."

"And I take it you think Jade's innocence is part of the truth," Miles said.

"Fuck yes, we do." Mei's eyes flashed.

"We do," Lemon said. "She's no killer."

"Good. As long as we agree. Neither is Felicia."

"I think we all agree," Hayley said.

"Agree to what?"

The voice came from behind them. Lemon whipped her head around. Caroline Timkins flashed just the smallest smile at her before turning a huge grin on Mei.

"Hey," Mei slid over to make room beside her. She patted the wood. "Glad you could make it."

Lemon's shock stuck in her throat. Why didn't Mei tell her she'd invited Caroline?

Caroline slid into the seat and shoved her hand across the table at Miles. "Hey, I'm Caroline."

"Miles." He shook it lightly before standing up. "And I gotta go see about a guy." He waved and disappeared into the flashing lights of the club.

Caroline shoved her hand at Hayley next, then turned her head, piercing the gaze of everyone at the table. "So, what are we talking about? What are we agreeing to?"

Lemon's chest tightened, but before she could figure out what to say, Mei stepped in. "Nothing important." She leaned toward Caroline, big, sweet grin on her face. "I'd rather talk about you."

Chapter Seven

The rectangular piece of Astroturf was covered in dogs. The crowd, way bigger than the usual Thursday afternoon size, was rowdy. The four dogs Lemon got paid to exercise plus two of her own three romped freely among the pack. The scene projected chaos in the most delightful of ways to the casual observer.

Wagging tails and pink tongues hanging out of smiling dog jowls gave most people a boost of oxytocin. But this many unpredictable personalities and sharp teeth in close proximity had a very different affect on Lemon. A Xanax would be welcome right about now because her anxiety was hitting the roof.

Neal's kind tone hit her ears before she saw his approach. "Hey, Lemon. How are you today?"

She pulled her gaze away from Klee's butt-sniffing adventures to greet her fellow dog-walker. "Hi Neal. Busy here today, huh?"

Neal leaned down. The bun perched on top of his head cantered precariously toward her. His voice took on the quality of a loud whisper. "New company found our place." He stuck his thumb over his shoulder. "This is one of six that come here now."

An age-old rivalry between small dog-walking businesses of one or two people and companies with multiple hired walkers doing large volume simmered within the low fences of dog parks across the city.

"Maybe we need to find a new place," Lemon suggested.

Neal shrugged. "There's a ton of great places, but most of my clients need a fence." As if to demonstrate, he dropped his hand on the metal behind her. It wobbled ominously. "Besides, I'd be afraid to go to Golden Gate Park, especially with Milo. I heard he found another body."

Lemon leaned against the cold metal at her back and sighed, her thoughts wandering to the Bassett Hound she'd left at home. He'd long since given up on the social niceties of the dog park, when she brought him all he ever did was curl up in a shady corner to take a nap. "Unfortunately, yes. The missing police officer."

"I heard. Bananas, right?"

Lemon swallowed. This case was so much more than interesting rumor to her. It was personal. "Definitely."

"So you were there with the police, then?"

As much as she liked Neal, she was in no mood to dish about this. She considered using the fullness of the dog park as an excuse to leave. She could take the dogs on leashes over to the Presidio. But Neal would likely just follow her. While trying to figure out her next move, she gave him a quick affirmation.

"Damn. You must have such a story to tell. Did you talk to any reporters about it? I've seen a lot of stuff, but only a tiny mention of Milo, and that was by the detective, what was his name…Zane…Zimmer…"

Lemon's ringing phone abruptly interrupted Neal's one-way conversation. "Sorry. I have to take this."

Neal smiled and waved, moving away from Lemon as she pulled the phone out of her pocket. Too grateful for the break to even bother looking at who is was, she just stuck it to her ear. "Hello."

"Lemon?"

"Yeah. Who is this?"

"It's Tony. Tony Jillian. We met a couple times, if you remember. I work with Jade. Not at the lab, but at the…our business."

She swallowed down her surprise. "Tony, hi. Of course I remember you." She knew Tony had her number because he and Jade needed to be able to get a hold of each other at all hours. But he had never before used it. "What's up?"

"My money troubles are real. I just wanted you to know that."

"Um, okay."

"Look, Lemon. I'm sure you've talked to Jade's parents. And I searched the Internet about that Andy guy. I know he's connected to your best friend's family. Can we just talk real for a minute here and leave all the bullshit out of it."

Lemon wanted to sink down and sit crisscross applesauce, but the likelihood that the patch of Astroturf beneath her feet was soaked in dog urine stopped her. Instead, she leaned against the fence and rested her elbow on the rail. "Yes, Tony. Of course."

"I really don't have the money. In fact, things are shittier than ever. I had to hire someone to help me with the business since Jade has been in jail."

"I hear you, Tony. And it doesn't matter anyway. She didn't get bail. There's no point in beating yourself up about it."

A loud whooshing breath traveled through the phone line. "Thanks, Lemon. I guess I'm just feeling a little defensive. Jade's mom has been calling me and basically traumatizing me on a regular basis."

"I'm sorry. And I get that. But I'm not judging you."

"You sure? I mean, Andy talked to me like I was suspect fucking number one. Which makes absolutely no sense. Why would I kill someone I barely know to put the person I fucking need to help me in jail? It makes no sense!"

"I hear you, Tony. I do."

"Okay, thanks." He let out a massive sigh. "The truth is, I want to help Jade. How can I do that?"

Coincidence slammed into Lemon. "Actually, I was wondering what you know about Jade's boss, Tammy."

"Tammy? What do you want to know about Tammy?"

"Well, we heard you were working with her just before you quit. And there's been some suggestion that maybe you didn't just quit to, you know, start the business. But that maybe she had something to do the reason you left?" Lemon flinched as soon as the words left her mouth.

But rather than come back at her with anger as she expected, Tony laughed. "So that's the rumor, huh? Well I'll tell you what, Lemon. I did leave to start the business. I wanted to be in charge of my-fucking-self and myself alone. I knew Jade could do the same, so she made a good partner. But getting away from Tammy was definitely a big bonus. We didn't get along. She's a pain-in-the-ass, to be honest."

"Wow, so that bad, huh?"

"It wasn't always. We were friends once. But that was before we worked closely together. Things kind of fell apart a couple years ago. Anyway, I'm not alone. No one at the lab likes her."

"Including Jade?"

"Jade's a pretty easy-going chick, but yeah, even her. I was constantly trying to convince her to leave and go full-time with me. If we can get her out of jail it may be her only choice." No joy echoed in his statement.

The now familiar knot in Lemon's stomach tightened. "Yeah. I guess so, huh? If you know Tammy pretty well, can I ask you a favor? Well, really it's for Jade."

"I will help Jade in anyway I can. As long as I don't have to deal with her parents. What do you need?"

"Can you get me the names of all the people in Tammy's life that are important to her."

"Sure. I can do that. And if I know that any of them have a connection to Jade or Berkeley, I'll mark that on the list, yeah?"

"That would be amazing! Thank you!"

"Sure. Keep your chin up, Lemon."

The phone line went dead. Lemon glanced up, a smile on her face. She felt as if she'd done something helpful. But her smile melted away as soon as she saw that one of her clients was rolling in a massive pile of dog poop.

****

"Preliminary autopsy finding is in, did you hear?"

The statement hit Lemon as soon as she stepped in the door. She hadn't even managed to get the dogs unhooked from their leashes yet. The cold from the foggy evening air still clung to her fur-covered clothing.

"Hey Caroline."

From her perch on a barstool sidled up to the kitchen island, Caroline waved. Across from her, Mei glanced up from the bowl of whatever she was whisking to throw Lemon a quick greeting.

Lemon managed to get Klee and Snickers unhooked. The two smaller dogs trudged to their beds, exhausted from their outing with a group of Mini Pinschers, Chihuahuas, and Schnauzers. Milo, who'd been spared the exuberant play, loped in the opposite direction, seeking out affection from his favorite person.

Lemon indulged in a few pats and a decent butt scritch for the hound before she headed over to sit down beside Caroline. "What's this about the autopsy now?"

Caroline raised a glass of wine. "Poison. Can you believe it?"

"Poison?" Lemon turned to exchange a glance with Mei. Had she heard right?

"I've been thinking about this," Mei said. "I mean, how does a victim of poison end up in full uniform in the bushes of the park with her gun thrown away? It makes no sense."

"No it doesn't."

"And they didn't find anything she could have eaten or drank with her body either," Caroline said. "No water bottle or thermos, or lunch bag. Nothing."

"Well, the killer obviously moved her. I'm sure they got rid of whatever they used to poison her as well," Mei said.

"Hold onto your hat," Caroline said, her eyes growing wider. "She wasn't moved."

"What do you mean she wasn't moved?" Lemon asked, unable to wrap her head around this revelation.

"I mean, she died right there in the bushes. That's it. That's where she died." Caroline dropped this bomb and took a long sip of her red wine.

Lemon stared at Caroline, dumbfounded. Only the sound of glass moving against granite gained her attention as Mei slid an offering of wine across the counter to her. Lemon scooped it up gratefully and took her own sip. The red was rich and fruity. A Pinot she'd guess. She took another sip and pondered the bizarre facts.

It made no sense. The very last thing she expected was poisoning. And she was certain the police were not prepared for this result either. A bullet to the head, knife wounds, even strangulation, all seemed plausible. But poisoning was a crime usually reserved for the home.

"Wow. That's just…"

"Bizarre," Caroline said. "I know."

"And they're sure she wasn't moved?" Mei asked.

Caroline glanced over her shoulder, her gaze briefly hitting Milo's sleeping form before turning back. "Well, there isn't any evidence that she was moved. Add that to Milo's…whatever…and Zahn is absolutely convinced."

"But you're not?" Mei asked.

Caroline rested her chin on her fist, her elbow propped on the counter. "I have to be honest. No. I don't see any evidence that Milo did anything more than get lucky. To pin something as important as location of death on his crazy trail across the park seems extremely tenuous to me."

A deeply uncomfortable silence blanketed the room, punctuated only by Milo's snoring.

"But, couldn't you be right *and* Milo be right?" Mei asked.

"What do you mean?"

"Well maybe he followed the scent in reverse. Like he followed the scent of the person who killed Berkeley from where they ditched her gun to where the body was hidden, you know, the reverse of how it happened."

Caroline pivoted on the barstool, this time blatantly staring at Milo as if she were giving him a thorough examination with nothing more than her eyes as a tool. Milo continued to snooze at Lemon's feet.

"I don't think so. He definitely needs real training. He just got lucky." Almost as an afterthought, she looked up at Lemon and said, "Sorry."

Lemon shrugged. Her urge to defend Milo's brilliance when it came to finding dead things sat right beside her desire for him to continue doing it.

"He's really good," Mei said. "I mean, I've seen him in action. I don't think he got lucky."

Caroline's eyes narrowed for a split second. The almost imperceptible action quickly morphed into a wide smile that affected her entire face. "Of course. Such raw talent. For sure. He just needs a little refinement is all."

The words drifted out of Lemon's mouth at the exact moment that the plan entered her head. "Can you help?"

"Help?" Caroline asked.

Even as she expressed the idea, Lemon wasn't entirely certain why. "Yeah, could you help me train him? You know, to be better."

Caroline's gaze ran over Lemon from head to toe before shifting back to Milo. Her nose wrinkled up as if she smelled something rotten. But by the time she turned back she plastered on a smug grin. "I can help. But you have to do everything I say, exactly as I say it."

"No problem." Mei, whose face jutted between them, smiled at Caroline, her eyelashes beating rapidly. "Lemon is good at taking instructions. She takes care of each and every one of the dogs she walks exactly the way their owners like."

"Pet parents," Lemon said.

Mei rolled her eyes. "Whatever. We can do it."

"We?" Lemon asked.

"Of course." Mei pierced Lemon with a wide-eyed glare. "You know I totally want to help. I'm super interested in dog training."

She was not. Her fear of dogs only recently abated, and Mei still only tolerated all but Snickers. Milo sat at the bottom of her list of favorites.

Caroline clapped her hands together. "Great! This will be fun."

Lemon wasn't sure about that. But she was certain of one thing, this little side adventure might lead them somewhere.

Chapter Eight

"Same rules apply. No touching. Prisoner remains cuffed. I stand here." The woman pointed to a well-worn section of tile beside the door in the tiny room. Her gaze stayed on Lemon. "Understand?"

Since Lemon had never visited a jail before, she wasn't at all certain what the rules usually were, but she smiled at the uniformed corrections officer. Only when she and Andy turned toward the little table crammed into the boxy room did she whisper her question. "Same as what?"

"You don't usually get a private room to meet with someone in jail, Lemon. Unless you're a lawyer." He winked. "And a lawyer's assistant."

Andy dropped into a sturdy metal chair and gestured for Lemon to sit beside him. Despite the presence of dusky grey padding, the seat was no more comfortable than a hard, wooden bench.

Lemon stared at an identical chair across the thin wooden table from them. Cold and empty, it sat waiting for Jade. Beside her, Andy rustled through a stack of papers he'd brought in. Originally shoved inside a manila envelope, they were now spread across the scarred surface of the small table in what looked to be a disorganized jumble.

The door created a loud squawking sound, gaining Lemon's full attention. Jade, with a second corrections officer walking so closely behind her their footfalls were necessarily in step, entered the room.

Shadowy bags hung below Jade's eyes, their usual sparkle dulled to a lifeless grey that nearly matched the chairs. Her mouth moved from a deep frown to a soft smile as she spotted Lemon. Her chin, pointed at the floor when she first stepped into the room, jutted up as she fell into the chair opposite them.

Jade pulled her hands up onto the table, the metal cuffs clinging to her wrists clanked as an ominous reminder of the situation. "Lemon." The word came out of her mouth as if it were a drop of relief, but the tenor of her voice was thick and strained.

Lemon reached across the table. But before her hand could make contact with Jade, the officer cleared her throat. Lemon glanced over at the woman and shivered in fear. She sat back in her chair, tucking her hands into her lap. "Hi Jade. Are you okay?"

Jade nodded. Nothing else. No words. As if lying could only be accomplished bodily, not verbally.

"Jade. You have to tell me if anything is going on at the jail I need to know about," Andy said.

"No, I'm good. Unharmed." The sadness in her voice filled the room and echoed back to them.

"Okay, well. Lemon has been helping me look into a few things, and we want to ask you some questions. Are you up for that?"

Jade straightened her spine. "Yes. Absolutely. It's nice to have visitors." She smiled at Lemon.

"I'm so sorry, Jade," Lemon said.

Jade frowned. A tear made its way slowly down her cheek. "You didn't frame me."

"No. But someone did," Andy said. "And we need to figure out who. One step at a time. Let's start with Felicia."

Jade's eyes moved back to Andy. "Yeah. Okay."

"She has a solid alibi."

"All right, so she's eliminated as a suspect?"

"Yes. But there's more. Lemon?"

Lemon tangled her fingers together in her lap. "We talked to her best friend, Miles. And he says she was trying to warn you about a guy named Galen

who was calling around looking for you. And that's why Felicia was following you that night. But that she never got the chance to tell you about it. Do you know anything about a Galen?"

"Galen? Yeah. I mean, kind of."

"Kind of how?"

"This is weird, and I don't know why I remember it, but Berkeley sent me a text one day, a few days before she went missing actually. And it made no sense at all. When I sent back the question mark text she said it was a mistake. She meant for it to go to Galen."

Andy scribbled something on one of the random sheets of paper spread out in front of him. "Uh huh. And did she say anything else about this person?"

"No. That was pretty much it. The end of the text exchange."

"What was the cryptic message meant for Galen, do you remember?"

"Sorry. No."

This case had a way of making Lemon feel like she was on a roller coaster. For each pull upward of anticipation and hope there was a corresponding downward fall into the abyss of the unknown.

"It's okay." Andy's kind voice bounced off the hard, cold walls of the tiny room. "We'll figure it out. Let me ask you about your business partner, Tony Jillian."

"Oh, geez. Andy, don't listen to my mom. Tony didn't murder Berkeley to frame me. That's just ridiculous."

Andy shot Jade a disarming smile, the same one Lemon had seen him use on both Jade's mother and Mei. "I met with him. He seems very nice."

"He's not nice. He's a ruthless businessman. He's dedicated and completely Type A. But he's no killer. And I'm more good to him out of here than in."

"I interviewed him, and my impression matched that. But I am still interested in exploring all his connections. Particularly those he and you have in common, like Tammy Ryder."

"Oh, Tammy." Jade slumped back in her chair. She brought her cuffed hands up to her face so she could reach one fingernail out and scratch her nose. "She's the reason I'm in here."

Andy cocked his head. "How so?"

"She identified my ID card as fake and the one in the bushes as real. Only there is no way that's possible."

"Why not? How do you know the one you had on your person was the real one?" Andy asked.

Lemon expected Jade to get angry at the accusation in the question. But she showed no malice as she answered him. "I pulled it out of my backpack right before I left for the crime scene."

"Your backpack. Why wasn't it on your person if you went from work to the crime scene?"

"After I get into the building, I stick my ID in my backpack while I work. If I don't, it ends up swinging around the lanyard on my neck and getting into the things I work on. My work is too delicate for that. I used to leave it on my desk, but I kept forgetting it when I went home and getting stuck outside the building the next morning. So I got in the habit of putting it my backpack."

Andy didn't peer up from the notes his hand frantically scribbled. "And where do you keep your backpack while you are working all day?"

"I usually throw it under my desk."

"Doesn't it get in the way of your feet as you work?"

"I don't sit at my desk much. I'm usually moving around the lab. Then I go back to my desk to enter things into the computer, but I rarely even sit down to do that. It's like, quick note then back to what I'm doing. You know. Sometimes, I just take the laptop around the room with me. The desk is basically a place to put things that don't have to be sterile."

"I see." Andy made a final scribble before leaning back in his chair. "Tell us about your relationship with Tammy."

"She's fine. I mean, I've had worse bosses."

"So, you get along with her?" Andy asked.

Jade shrugged. "That might be too strong a statement."

Lemon remembered a few of the times an exhausted Jade told her about some her boss's harsh words during a long, double shift. "I thought she sounded pretty tough."

"Yeah, she was tough. But I could take it."

"But Tony couldn't?" Andy asked.

"Well, that was different."

"Different how?"

Jade stared at Andy. "He didn't tell you?"

"Tell me what?" Andy asked.

"That he and Tammy were once an item?"

"No. He definitely didn't. I take it, it ended badly?"

"Oh, for sure. He claimed she never got over her ex. At first she told him that she and her ex were just best friends. And he was like, well I don't want to be a dick and say she can't have male friends. And then things were weird, fishy, you know. They seemed to flirt all the time. So he brought it up again, and Tammy made him feel like an asshole by telling him her ex was trans, and he needed support. So he backed off again. But then I guess he caught them in a compromising position, and that was it. So they broke up, and he quit his job."

"Was she mad that you partnered with him on the business?" Lemon asked. She couldn't help but think that might be a natural reaction for someone to have.

Jade shrugged, the action causing the metal of her handcuffs to scrape against the wood with a shiver-inducing sound. "She never said anything about it. Though she was real hesitant to let me off work on time after she found out. She always had some excuse for me to work overtime. Tony thought it was retribution for working with him."

"But you aren't so sure?" Andy asked.

A deep sadness took over Jade's face. "I'm not sure of anything anymore."

Lemon gripped her hands together, resisting the urge to reach out to Jade.

"Hey," Andy said, his voice soft and smooth. "We'll figure it out. Me and Lemon and Mei."

Jade smiled weakly. "And Milo. Don't forget Milo."

A swell of unwelcome anticipation filled Lemon's belly. She loved her pup, but she lived in fear of things he uncovered in dark places.

****

"Look, I wouldn't normally ask this, but as a lawyer, it's my job to be nosey and find out everything I can. And I think it might help to know what happened between you and Jade." Andy's left cheek bowed out in a circle filled with crab cakes as he pointed his plastic fork at Lemon.

Lemon shifted on the wooden picnic table that sat between the square configuration of food trucks. Her own falafel sat quietly in front of her, waiting for her to dig in. "I mean, how does that help?"

"Anything can come up in court. And I don't like surprises."

Lemon let out a thick breath. "Okay. It's all my fault. Or my hang-up really."

"What kind of hang-up."

"Death. I hate it."

Andy chuckled. "You're not alone there, kiddo."

"Yeah, well. I was never cut out for your job or Detective Zahn's."

"Or Jade's?"

"Definitely not Jade's."

"So you fought over her sharing the grim details?"

"Not really. No. I mean, we didn't fight. It was…"

"Yeah?"

Lemon stabbed the falafel with her fork. "So my dog likes dead things."

Andy didn't seem phased by the random change in subject. He dropped his fork and folded his hands in front of him. "Yeah. So I've heard."

"And so I've had some unpleasant experiences thanks to him."

"Like finding Jillian Ross's feet outside the Legion of Honor?"

Lemon swallowed hard. "Yeah. Exactly. And so I know that smell, you know."

"Hmmm. Mmmm."

"And one night…Jade and I were…intimate…and um…"

"Let me guess," Andy said, saving her from actually having to say the words. "She smelled like death. Left over from work."

"Yeah. And it kind of… you know…killed my libido."

"So she showered, and…"

"Didn't matter. It was kind of, in there, you know. And things got weird from there. And we decided to take a break. And that's it."

Andy leaned back and slapped his hands on the table between them. "I understand."

"You do?"

"Sure. It's a basic problem of sex drive. And without it, it's hard to maintain a burgeoning relationship. And I'm sure it hurt her feelings, which made you feel guilty, which only exacerbated the issue. And on and on it went."

Lemon's gaze was pinned to the table. "Yeah." She shoved half a falafel in her mouth and chewed slowly, the action reflecting her pain.

"Lemon," Andy said, drawing her gaze. "It's not that bad. Just a snag. And not that unusual of one. I had a client once who hated the way her firefighter husband smelled for days after a fire. Didn't matter how much he showered."

The glimmer of hope his words ignited was quickly quelled by the realization of what he said. "Wait. A client of yours?"

"Oh. Yeah." Andy turned back to his crab cakes. "She killed him."

Chapter Nine

Lemon wasn't sure what it was about this dog park and Tony Jillian. She'd been standing right here the first time he called her, and she was in the same spot, leaned against the concrete wall watching Hubert, a middle-aged Pug, take a poop when she got an email from Tony.

Lemon,
I got that list of people associated with Tammy ready for you. I have linked to their social media profiles where possible. Please let me know what else I can do. And keep me posted!
Thanks,
Tony

Lemon scrolled down the long list. There had to be thirty or forty names there. Other than a few of Jade's co-workers that Lemon recognized, most of them were complete strangers. Until her eyes landed on one very significant name.

Galen Ryan.

Galen. She'd definitely heard that name before. It was the name Felicia mentioned. The person that was calling around for Jade. Felicia hadn't mentioned a last name, but how many Galens could there be in a tight circle of acquaintances in San Francisco?

She stared at the screen. It was one of the few names without an associated link to a social media profile. A quick Internet search turned up just one article about a Galen Ryan in the Bay Area. The rest were all in Ireland. She glanced up at the dogs, and finding them perfectly content, returned her focus to the phone. She hit the link and waited.

The article that came up read:

Trans Man Speaks Out About Career Equity
What if you were completely qualified, borderline over-qualified for a job? You have a stellar resume. You give a killer interview. Then you get a call from HR. They've been looking into you and can't find evidence of your existence prior to ten years ago. You have to tell them

you changed your name. They insist on knowing what your old name was. Say its essential to getting your background done. So you tell them. You tell them your dead name. The name that is the wrong gender, the wrong name for you. Two days later, you receive an email saying they've chosen someone else for the job.

That's exactly what happened to Galen Ryan. At nineteen, he embraced who he was and started his transition. By thirty he was happy, healthy, and had a degree and a slew of experience to prove he could take on any private investigation a professional agency might need.

But he couldn't seem to get a job.

Because they all found out he was transgender and decided to pass.

Even in San Francisco. Even here. Transphobia happens every day.

Galen did not disclose his current career, only that he works for himself. He was certain to let us know he was happy and successful. But his road wasn't easy.

It's a reminder to us all to be kind, to be open-minded. To be inclusive. Transphobia might just lose you the best employee you never had.

Lemon ripped herself away from the phone to check on the pups. Snickers was chasing Killer—a tiny Yorkie—in a tight circle. Julie was attempting to steal a tennis ball from Bobby, who had no interest in letting her get it. And Hubert napped by the water bowl.

Galen Ryan called Felicia looking for Jade. He was on Tony's list of people associated with Tammy. And he had a mysterious profession that was presumably associated with investigation work.

It was a lot to unpack.

Lemon's eyes dropped down to the screen again. She was about to close out the article when she saw a link at the bottom.

Connect to Gaylen on social media at bayareadudeandhisdog.

Lemon hit the link. It took her to a social media account with lots of pictures of Galen and his dog.

Deeply good-looking, Galen posed with an equally photogenic pitty-mix sporting a wide, goofy smile in pic after pic.

She checked the comments on a few pictures. Most talked about how cute the dog—whose name was apparently Tiger—looked and how great Galen looked. But Lemon's scrolling came to a complete stop when she came across a picture of Galen and Tiger at a dog park. But not just any dog park. The one Lemon stood in at that very moment.

Scrolling frantically, Lemon slogged through all the comments. Her eyes scanned for something specific. And there it was.

A friend named FredAny's message said, *We love it there. Maybe we'll run into you.*

And Galen responded, *That would be awesome. We're there every Tuesday and Thursday around 4-ish.*

There it was. A plan hatched. A diabolical scheme created. And Lemon planned to keep it to herself. No one would know what she had in mind until she left this very piece of urine soaked astroturf with some real, concrete evidence.

****

Three hours later, Lemon was back at the dog park being interrogated.

"What are you doing at the dog park? I thought you went to the Presidio on Thursday afternoons. You have all those big dogs. They need to stretch their legs."

How her mother had become an expert on dog needs, Lemon wasn't sure. But she wasn't going to let her freak-out from thousands of miles away in Belize stop Lemon from stalking Galen Ryan and his adopted pitty-mix.

"Kelsey had surgery last week. She's not up for a long walk yet." This was actually true, which is why she'd let Kelsey out to pee and then put her back in her crate before heading to the dog park with the rest of her charges.

"Oh. Poor baby. I can't believe they take out their entire uterus."

"Mom. We're not having this strange spay conversation again. I gotta go watch the dogs. Love you. Talk to you next week."

She waited for her mom to hang up before shoving the phone in her pocket and scanning the dog park. The place was practically deserted, and she knew why Galen chose this time to come. Dog parks, like many places in the Bay Area, suffered an ebb and flow of visitors. Finding that sweet spot between crowds was a gift.

Her five clients were literally alone in the park. She'd brought Milo along as well, just in case. If Milo showed undue interest in Galen,

Lemon had no idea if that actually meant something, but it was worth a try, right?

A half hour passed before the creak of the gate signaled a new arrival. Lemon swung her head to the right. As if in slow motion, he walked in, a brindle dog right at his heels. His hair tossed in the wind just so, framing the sharp angles of his face.

Lemon suppressed a shiver. Galen was objectively hot. She would need to get over that as well as the nerves pinging through her veins, reminding her that she was no expert in interrogating people about murder.

Seeing her deep stare, Galen waved at her, a friendly smile briefly flashed across his face before his attention returned to his dog, who loped happily across the space, tongue out, smile on.

Galen settled far enough away from Lemon that she had no way to approach casually. She'd have to rely on the dogs to create an opening. Luckily, Skip, the Husky mix, was never one to let a potential new friend pass him by. He marched over to the pitty, tongue out, tail on full wag.

Galen's dog took the bait, and after a long butt-sniffing session, they began to play. Hercules, a giant mutt of completely unknown origins, joined in the fun, causing his shadow, Marley, to reluctantly participate as well. Milo watched them all from a shady spot by the water bowl.

This was the opening. Lemon moved casually toward Galen, her eyes trained on the dogs, as if she were only moving to get a better view. Then she settled on the lone bench in the park, which happened to be within spitting distance of where Galen stood, arms crossed over his chest.

She slumped down with a sigh as if she were deeply exhausted. "I'm glad they made friends."

Galen glanced over at her quickly before returning his focus to the dogs. "Yeah. I usually come here when it's empty. Avoid the other dogs."

Ouch. Damn. He wasn't exactly Mr. Congenial was he? "Oh. Sorry."

Galen glanced back at her, his blue eyes catching hers. "Oh. No. Sorry. That was rude. He took a step toward her. "It's just because Tiger plays rough." He gestured toward Tiger and Skip, who were in all out wrestling match. "And he scares the crap out of the little dogs. It always ends up with someone snatching up a little Chihuahua as if they think he's going to eat them and yelling at me about my big monster." He let out of a half huff, half chuckle. "Actually really happy to run into your crew. You a dog walker?"

Lemon's stomach fluttered. Success flew close. "Yeah. I usually take these big guys to the Presidio to stretch their legs, but I thought I'd try this out today. I just don't have the energy. You know?"

Galen sat on the opposite end of the bench. "I know what you mean. I don't know how you do it. I'm exhausted just watching them." He gestured toward the dogs. His forearm, exposed below where his shirt bunched at the elbow, sported a bright trans flag, beautifully inked as if it were flowing in the wind.

"It builds you know. Monday through Wednesday feels easy. By Thursday I'm dying. And by Friday I'm dead."

His laugh was deep and rich. "I hear that. You have your own dogs, too?"

Lemon pointed to the lazy Bassett Hound in the corner. "That one is mine."

"He seemed very chill."

"He can be. Unless he's on the scent of something. Then watch out."

"Huh. Poor dude."

"He's alright. He'd rather be here than left at home with the other two. He prefers people to other dogs."

Galen swiveled his head, squinted in the sun to look at her. "Mine is the exact opposite. But I love him. Wouldn't trade him."

"Is he a rescue?"

"Yeah. I got him—"

The entire conversation came to an abrupt end as the loud squeak of the gate stole their attention. They both turned to see a man in a full three-piece suit walk through.

A suit in San Francisco was rare enough. Not even in the Financial District did people usually dress that high end. But in SOMA, where millionaires wore hoodies, it was rarer still. And at a dog park situated under an overpass?

But that wasn't even the strangest thing about the visitor. He had no dog.

Galen shot out of his seat. "Hey. What are you doing here?"

The man's dark brown eyes drifted to Lemon for the briefest moment before pinning back on Galen. "Looking for you."

"Oh. Uh." Galen glanced at Lemon for a fraction of a second before shouting to Tiger. Regardless of his clear desire to stay, Tiger ran back to his dad and suffered through having his harness connected.

Galen stood, leash looped over one hand and waved at Lemon. "Nice talking with you. Hopefully they'll get to play again."

He followed the man toward the entrance to the park and Lemon felt her opportunity slipping away. "We'll be here on Tuesday, too," she called.

"Great. See you then." It was the last words she heard before he slipped through the gate and out of her grasp.

****

Whatever miracle had occurred, Lemon wasn't about to take it for granted. Mei woke up early on Friday morning and took the dogs out to pee before getting ready for work. This magical occurrence left Lemon with the rare opportunity to lounge in bed.

Sadly, she wasted most of it scrolling through random shit on her phone. She was about to toss it aside when she glanced at the text from Andy.

Next assignment—Caroline Timkins. Don't tell Mei. I think they are hooking up.

Lemon sat upright in the bed as if she'd just felt an earthquake. What was this? She immediately wrote back.

How did she come up?

Andy responded quickly. *Jade put her on the list of people Berkeley knew. Which makes sense since they are both cops. But if my niece is going to be hanging out with her, I want her looked into first thing. Are you good?*

Lemon bit her lip. Keeping something like this from Mei wouldn't be easy. But Andy wasn't the only one who felt protective of Mei.

I'm on it. I got this.

Awesome. Thanks.

Lemon deleted the texts before pulling herself out of bed. She was headed for the bathroom when she heard Mei shout from the living room. "Lemon. Get in here. Now!"

Bolting through the door, Lemon nearly fell face first onto the worn carpet of the hallway as her foot slammed down on a partially eaten dog bone. Limping and cursing, she made her way down the stretch into the living room and dropped onto the couch beside Mei.

"Look!" Mei pointed at the television with the remote.

The man has been identified as Galen Ryan, a private contractor who lives in the city.

Lemon's breath caught in her throat as the image of a black body bag, fully zipped and secured, was loaded into a truck.

At this time, authorities say they are not ruling out a hate crime. Mr. Ryan was a trans man and was recently featured in the media about his journey. Fortunately, his dog was unharmed and is in the care of friends.

The story turned to something about crab season, and Lemon swung around to face Mei. "What the hell happened?"

Her eyes just as wide and frantic as Lemon's, Mei practically shouted back, "He got shot. Isn't that the guy Andy mentioned?"

Lemon's stomach lurched. "I literally talked to him yesterday."

"What?" Mei shouted. "He was literally shot yesterday! When did you talk to him?"

"At the dog park."

Mei dropped her hands on Lemon's shoulder and leaned toward her. "You saw Galen Ryan at the dog park?"

"Yeah, the one in SOMA."

Mei's eyes seemed to pulse. "What time?"

"Um." The dryness in her throat created a block in her windpipe. Lemon couldn't breathe.

"Think Lemon."

"Last crew." It was all she could get out.

Mei bit her lip and swiveled her gaze to the ceiling. "Okay. So. Around 4 o'clock then. You usually leave to start getting them all at 3. Then you had to get all the way over to SOMA and park. And they are all due home by 5:30. So 4?"

"Yeah. Um. Probably. We were there for a while before he showed up."

"And you talked?"

"Yeah. But not about anything real. Only the dogs got along, and we were going to meet there again on Tuesday, which I thought would be good since, you know, we're supposed to be investigating him."

Mei leaned back on the couch as if she were deflating a balloon. "Oh my God, Lemon. He was killed around 5 o'clock last night just a few blocks away from the park."

"Oh wow."

"Oh wow is right! Lemon, you might have been hurt."

"No. No." Lemon held up her hand. There was something far more important here. "I might have seen the killer."

Chapter Ten

"So you met with a sketch artist?" Andy rubbed his chin with the back of his hand.

"Yeah. But honestly, I didn't get that great of a look at his face."

"You practically have a photographic memory. I'm sure you did a good job," Mei said.

Lemon shrugged. All weekend she'd been beating herself up over that moment in the dog park. She'd been so focused on the stranger's clothes and her lost chance to talk more with Galen that she'd barely glanced at his face. Having stared a killer in the eye and let him go was not high on her list of favorite things.

"I assume you talked to Zahn?" Andy asked.

"Yeah."

"Does this guy work every murder in San Francisco or something," Mei asked. "I mean, he said Berkeley's death was his top priority, and now he's working a random shooting in SOMA."

"It's not random. Remember, we have reason to believe Berkeley and Galen may have known each other."

"But Jade didn't know Galen," Mei said.

Andy dropped his hand on the table between them. The sound echoed through the small diner but went unnoticed as it joined all the other cacophonous sounds. "No. There's something there. I just don't know what yet. Zahn questioned Jade again. I was with her, but he really didn't say much. All I got out of the whole thing is that they found something with Galen's body."

"Ugh." Mei said. "Not again!"

"Yeah. Again."

"Please tell me it isn't yet another copy of Jade's work ID."

"Well that seems unlikely, but honestly, I have no idea what they found. I tell you what I am sure of." He eyed Lemon and Mei closely. "You two are out."

"What?" Mei and Lemon spoke at the same time.

He leaned over, his elbows planted on the woodgrain of the flimsy table. "You," he pointed to Lemon, "were within blocks and minutes of a murder after talking to the victim. That is not happening again. You're done. You're both done. This thing is too hot."

"No way, Uncle!" Mei said. "You need us."

"Jade needs us," Lemon said.

"I will get someone else. I'll pay for it out of my own pocket. I'll figure it out."

"No way. You can't do that," Mei said.

"Oh yes, I can. I am running this train and I'm not about to end up with one of you hurt. Not to mention if your mother knew any of this, Mei, we'd all be dead already."

"You need us," Lemon said. "We know all the players. We're already in. Remember what we were able to find out about Felicia. Just like that." She snapped her fingers. "No one else can get what we can so fast."

Andy paused. They had created an opening. Mei pounced. "And this thing with Galen was nothing but a coincidence. Lemon happened to take her clients to the same place. So what? The city is only eight by eight miles, technically tiny. It could totally happen. It did happen."

Guilt blossomed in Lemon's stomach, the product of another secret. She'd never revealed that she purposely went there to talk to Galen. Yes, she'd given Andy Tony's list with Galen's name on it, but with careful nonchalance, as if it meant nothing to her. They didn't know she'd gone there on purpose.

Andy remained silent.

"Come on, Uncle. Give us the next name to investigate. Let's just keep going."

Andy stared at Mei. Lemon shifted in her seat. Keeping Andy's request that she look into Caroline a secret, was another weight added to her heavy shoulders. One she wouldn't reveal now even if everything else fell away.

"Just give us someone safe to look into," Lemon said.

Andy shook his head. "I don't even know what safe is anymore."

"Tammy," Mei said. "We're not done looking into Tammy Ryder."

Andy's gaze flicked between Lemon and Mei. "Yeah. Okay. Keep looking at Tammy." He glanced down at his watch. "Shit. It's almost time." He stood quickly, causing the chair beneath him to scrape against the polished concrete.

"Time for what?" Mei asked.

Andy threw a tip on the table, hefted his messenger bag over his shoulder, and gestured for them to follow him as he pivoted on his heel and headed for the door. "Come on."

Mei and Lemon exchanged confused glances before practically tripping over the furniture to follow him. They all plunged out into a sunny afternoon. Andy's long legs moved smoothly down the sidewalk and skipped over a curb as he jaywalked across the street.

Mei followed at his heels, while Lemon got stuck, afraid of an oncoming truck. Once across the street, she jogged to catch up with them both. She reached them just as they settled at a bench at the edge of a grass-covered park. Mei patted the spot beside her. Lemon plopped down and sucked in her breath.

Andy pulled a tablet from his bag and started to play with it. What the hell was going on? And why wasn't Mei asking?

He glanced up and stared across the space. "Oh shit. It's at City Hall." He pointed to the building, whose dome could be seen in the distance. "Let's go see in person, shall we?" Andy shot up.

"See what?" Lemon practically shouted, her frustration breaking through.

"Press conference, about the Galen Ryan case." Andy glanced down at his watch. "We should have enough time. Come on."

Before Lemon and Mei were even off the bench, Andy had the tablet shoved back into his bag, and he loped across the grass. They both scrambled to keep up.

Andy didn't use sidewalks and crosswalks. He took the "as the crow flies" approach to reaching his destination. Grass, curbs, streets, honking cars, near death experiences with electric scooters, and a big muddy patch on one of the shortcuts were all ignored as he marched toward his destination.

Lemon felt as though she'd been through the city's blender of terror when they pulled up beneath the regal dome of the city hall building. By the looks of it, the press conference was just getting started. Lemon, Andy, and Mei squeezed into a spot on the sidewalk below the wide steps, pushing into a hole left by rival news agencies unwilling to get too close to one another.

"On behalf of the city, I want to express our deep concern for the murder of a transgender person. The mayor is out of town today, but she wanted me to convey how seriously we are taking this matter. We will do everything we can to ensure this crime is handled efficiently and effectively. I'm going to hand this over to Chief Mayfield in a moment." The speaker's starched black suit signaled that he was a civilian of some sort, most likely a PR person with the city. "But first I want to remind everyone that both the murder of Mr. Ryan and that of Officer Hyatt are part an active investigation."

The air hitting the back of Lemon's throat stung. Andy was right. SFPD had connected Galen and Berkeley's murders. This could be very good for Jade. It must be, right? Jade had the best possible alibi for the time of Galen's murder.

"For this reason," the man continued. "After the Chief speaks, I will be fielding questions based on what can and cannot be discussed in order to preserve the integrity of the ongoing investigation."

The man moved aside and Chief Mayfield stepped up to the podium. She adjusted the microphone with a smooth, practiced hand before speaking clearly into it. "First, I will be speaking about the shooting death that occurred yesterday in SOMA West. Galen Ryan, an independent contractor, was shot twice with a handgun at approximately 4:55 yesterday afternoon. Neighbors heard the shots and went to Mr. Ryan's aide, but no one got a good look at the shooter. Despite the efforts of bystanders and first responders, Mr. Ryan died on site. Mr. Ryan has been positively identified, and his family has been notified of his death. The San Francisco Police Department is determined to quickly solve this case and make an arrest. We take the death of all of our citizens, including our transgender citizens, very seriously. We are dedicated to finding Mr. Ryan's killer and bringing them to justice."

The chief coughed awkwardly into her fist. "The motive does not appear to be robbery. Mr. Ryan was found with an item on his person. This morning we connected that item to the death of Officer Berkeley Hyatt, whose body was found last week in Golden Gate Park."

A murmur ran through the crowd. Chief Mayfield lifted her hand. "We have been able to connect the two murders and intend to follow this lead. I cannot go into detail about what we found or how it connects the murders, but I would like to reiterate that we are confident that we have the right person in custody for Berkeley Hyatt's death, and we will soon have someone in custody for Galen Ryan's murder. Anyone with any information, should come forward."

"This doesn't even make sense," Mei said.

"No," Andy said. "They have to say more than that."

The chief stepped back and the guy in the suit took her place at the microphone. He didn't readjust it, he simply leaned forward speak into it. "We will take a few questions now."

He called a reporter in the front who, thankfully, asked the obvious question. "So, if Jade Milan was in jail yesterday, and you think she killed Officer Hyatt, how can Mr. Ryan's death be related?"

As if she expected that question—and based on the strange half-smile planted on her face, she did—the chief stepped back up to the microphone. "The object found with Mr. Ryan has been confirmed to belong to a close associate of Jade Milan."

Lemon met Mei's eyes. Shock stilled them both.

"It can't be you," Andy said. "In fact, its definitely not."

Lemon ripped her gaze away from Mei. Andy was staring at his phone, his brow furrowed up. "I just got a text from Fred. Detective Zahn just left their house."

"And?" Mei asked.

But Andy didn't get a chance to answer her before another reporter piped up. "Chief, you can't just drop a bomb like that and leave it there. What is this object? Who does it belong to? Have you arrested them?"

"No arrest has been made, yet. We've spoken to the person of interest, but we are not yet ready to make an arrest."

The guy in the suit stepped back up and held up his hands. "That's it for now. We'll be in touch."

Lemon turned to Andy. "What the hell was that?"

"You're not going to believe this."

The silence of the crowd around them morphed in a clattering of equipment being moved and conversation resuming. "What?" Mei practically shouted over the din.

Andy's head snapped up. Lemon followed his gaze. They'd gained the attention of people they did not want overhearing their conversation. "Come on. Let's move."

Once again Lemon found herself chasing Andy's long-legged stride across streets and through alleyways until they reached a parking garage. As they ducked into a concrete structure and the smell of wet cement pummeling them, he finally spoke. "I gotta head to San Rafael. I can drop you both off at home on the way."

"Wait." Mei grabbed his elbow. "What is going on?"

"The object found with Galen Ryan's body is a necklace. A necklace that belongs to Marla Milan. Her name is etched in the back of the heart pendant. It was a gift from Fred."

"What?" Mei and Lemon spoke at the exact same moment, fear and confusion punctuating their twin voices.

"Believe me, I am just as confused as you are. But I'm going to get to the bottom of this. Please get in the car."

"Oh we're getting in the car," Mei said as she pulled open the door. "But we are not going home. We're coming with you."

****

Lemon noticed that Marla Milan had squeezed her hands together so tightly her knuckles turned a cold shade of white. Beside her, perched at the edge of the couch, Fred's lips were pinched, creating a similar color palate. Lemon sat across from them beside Mei, her own hands gripped to her sides. Andy was on a chair that looked so stiff and hard Lemon had avoided it like the plague when she'd first entered the room. But Andy had pulled it into the center room and perched on it regally as he proceeded to run the show.

"Okay start with the visit from Detective Zahn," Andy said to Marla and Fred. "He came over. You didn't call me right away. Why not?"

"Because we thought it was just a visit asking for details. You know, things that could help find the real killer," Fred said.

Andy ran a hand through his hair. It fanned up like a physical flag reflecting his stress. "Okay. Listen, always call me. No matter what. Okay?"

Fred's gaze hit the floor.

"Was he alone?"

"No. He had a partner with him. A woman," Fred said. "He introduced her, but I don't remember her name."

"Okay. What happened when you invited them in? Did they look around? Did they touch anything?"

Fred shook his head. Marla remained uncommonly still and silent beside him. "He just came in and sat down. His partner stood right there. Never sat." Fred pointed to the end of the couch. "We offered them drinks. He took an iced tea, she didn't. And then he started asking if we'd heard about the murder in San Francisco yesterday afternoon."

"And had you?"

"No. We actually hadn't. So he told us about it. I told him it was sad and all, but I couldn't figure out what it had to do with us or with Jade. Then he brings out this necklace all wrapped up in a plastic bag."

Marla let out a sob.

"And it was Marla's necklace?" Andy asked.

"Yep," Fred said.

Lemon felt her stomach lurch.

"And he said it was found with this man's dead body." Fred's voice cracked.

"Okay, so when was the last time you saw the necklace?" Andy asked.

Marla wiped at her eyes with a fistful of tissues and glanced up. Her gaze moved to Lemon and Mei briefly before landing on Andy. "Two days ago. I took it to the pawn shop on 4th street along with some other jewelry. I sold it all to get money to help Jade."

Andy stood quickly, the fluid movement buzzing through the room. "Do you have the receipt?"

Marla stood as well, though she moved slower, as if every part of her was in pain. Lemon's stomach hurt just watching her. "Come with me, I'll get it for you."

The two of them headed down the hallway, leaving Mei, Lemon, and Fred to stare at each other. "So." Mei broke the silence. "Fred. Did you ever meet Jade's boss at the crime lab? Tammy, I think her name is."

Lemon nearly rolled her eyes at the feigned innocence in Mei's voice as she pretended not to remember Tammy's name.

"Um, I think so," Fred said. "Maybe at an event." He rubbed his forehead with the back of his hand.

Lemon felt sorry for Fred. Everything he was going through had to be so deeply overwhelming it was hard to think, let alone remember random people you only met once or twice. "Like a work picnic?" she suggested.

Fred dropped his hand in his lap and stared at Lemon. "Yes, only it wasn't official. It was more like a party for someone…wait, I remember. It was for Tony. It was his retirement party when he left the lab to go full-time into the business. Only he didn't really retire, I don't think. Not sure he's actually old enough for that. Or maybe he is. I don't know. But, anyway, it was his party."

"And Tammy was there?" The tone of Mei's voice as she asked the question unveiled her surprise.

"Yeah. Of course. She's the boss of the lab. Why wouldn't she be there?" Fred asked.

Mei looked to Lemon, her gaze practically begging for support. Lemon sighed. Why did she always have to be the one to get Mei out of her verbal binds? She plunged ahead. "It's just that Tony implied he wasn't really on good terms with Tammy when he left. Like maybe she was mad at him for leaving."

"The boss never likes it," Fred said. "But they have to show up and smile. It's part of the job. I've done it myself a time or two."

"So she seemed happy that day?" Mei asked.

Fred shrugged. "I really don't remember. Sorry."

"It's totally fine," Lemon said. "We're just wondering about Tammy is all."

Fred ran a hand over his cheek. "You should ask Jade about her."

"Great idea," Lemon said. "We'll do that."

Mei pressed her lips together and sat back on the couch. A few beats of awkward silence separated the end of the conversation and the moment Andy and Marla emerged from the hallway.

Andy held a small piece of pink paper in his hand. He waved it at Lemon and Mei. "Come on, ladies. We have a pawn broker to see."

Chapter Eleven

Lemon wrinkled her nose. Though not quite as bad as the smell of a dead squirrel dug up and delivered with pride to her by Milo, the odor permeating the pawn shop was still mildly offensive.

The man behind the glass counter wore a disarming grin perched under a floppy mop of wavy blonde hair that half hid his eyes. "What can I do for ya?"

Andy matched his approachability with an affable smile. "Can I talk to you about Mrs. Milan? I'm her lawyer."

The man turned from a pale shade of white to ghostly. "Oh, um, that. I heard about that."

"Thought you probably did. Did the police call you?"

"Just left actually." He pointed to the door. "About ten minutes ago."

"And?"

The man held up his hands in surrender. "I gave them the pawn paperwork I had. All of it."

Andy leaned over, his arms resting on the glass case, shadowing over a set of thick gold and silver chains on display below. "Great. Then I suppose that includes the information about who you sold Mrs. Milan's necklace to?"

"I…I didn't."

"What do you mean, you didn't?"

"She didn't sell it to me. She pawned it. She has the ticket."

"Yeah, she showed me. But if it was pawned it should be safe and sound in your back room waiting for her to pay back the loan and retrieve the item. Only there's at least one piece of her jewelry that isn't back there, isn't that right?"

"The rest is. I'll show you." The man popped the latch on a waist high door to his right and held it open in invitation. "Come on. I'll show you what I showed the detective."

Andy's brow furrowed, but he followed the man. Mei and Lemon stayed close at his feet like a couple of ducklings following safely behind mom. They entered a brightly lit storeroom, rows of overhead florescent lights beamed off tall metal shelves packed with items, each with a bulky tan tag attached to it using a thin strip of string or a tab of tape.

Lemon squinted against the assault on her retinas from the bright lights as she tried to parse out how one could find anything in this vault of items, all randomly stacked on shelves in haphazard fashion.

But the shopkeeper had no trouble. Though that could be because he was just there moments before with Detective Zahn. They followed him as he snaked through the uneven rows of surrendered objects until he came to an abrupt stop in the middle of a row near the back of the seemingly endless room.

He snatched a shoebox off the shelf and opened it. Inside were several sandwich bags, each containing a necklace, ring, or pair of earrings. All gleamed with gold, diamonds, and sapphires. "I gave her good money for it all. And it's all here, except that necklace with her name on it. The one the cops had."

"How exactly did the necklace get out of here." Andy pointed at the box. "And over at a crime scene in SOMA?"

The man snapped the box shut and shoved it back into its place on the shelf. "I wish I knew."

"Is that what you told the cops?"

"Basically, yeah."

There was something deeply wrong with this.

"What kind of security do you have here?" Andy asked.

"The best. If you're thinking someone burglarized me, think again. First, nothing else is missing. Second, I have cameras everywhere." He pointed to the ceiling where a black globe stared down at them. "I would know. And I'm telling you that since I obtained the necklace, no one has broken in."

"Sorry to ask this." Andy tucked one thumb into the belt loop of his slacks. His cheeks pinked, which impressed Lemon since she was sure it was all an act. "But any of your staff?"

"Nope. Sure of it. The only staff that's been back here in the past couple days was Jacob, my son." The man glared at Andy with a look that dared him to accuse his own flesh and blood of such a crime. "And he only worked for a couple hours yesterday."

Risking what Lemon was sure was life and limb, Andy asked. "But he was back here?"

"Yep. With a cop." The man thrust his chin up.

"A cop? A different cop than the one you just spoke to?"

"Happens all the time. Police want to see an item or our records about one. Usually they're looking for fenced goods. But we take plenty of precautions. You won't find any of that here."

"So, tell me about the cop your son brought back here, what was he looking for?" Andy asked.

The man shrugged. "Don't know. Jacob didn't say."

"Do you think I could talk to Jacob?"

"You're a lawyer. Why don't you just ask the cops what they wanted?"

Andy smiled. "I'm a defense attorney."

The man chuckled. "Alright. I'll let you know. You got a card?"

Andy pulled a small business card out of the pocket of his shirt and handed it to the man between two of his fingers. "Please. Have him call me."

"Yeah. I will."

"Any chance you have video of the police and Jacob I could see?"

"'Fraid not. The police asked Jacob to turn off the cameras when they got here."

"Is that standard practice?"

The man just shrugged in response and led them back out to the lobby of his store. A couple lingered by a set of guitars. The man waved at Andy, Mei, and Lemon before jogging over to the couple with a wide smile. "Lookin' for a guitar?"

Lemon's feet felt heavy as they moved over the tile floor to follow Andy and Mei out of the glass doors. The sun struck her eyes as she stepped onto the sidewalk. "What do we do now?"

Andy didn't stop to contemplate her question, his long legs continued to move toward the car. "As for this." He hooked his thumb over his shoulder, pointing at the rapidly retreating pawn shop. "We wait for Jacob to call."

"And if he doesn't." Lemon's anxiety heightened. She hated to rely on this man's sketchy son for evidence.

Whatever Jade suffered would only be made worse if her mother landed in a cell beside her. The nightmare continued to spin out of control, and Lemon felt compelled to do something about it, even if she had no clue what that was.

"He will," Andy said confidently. "And if he doesn't, I'll come back every single day until I talk to him. I want to know who this supposed cop was that stole the necklace."

"You think a cop stole the necklace?" Out of breath from keeping up with Andy's pace, Mei sounded as shocked by the revelation as Lemon did.

"I think someone who presented themselves to Jacob as a cop stole the necklace, yes." Andy stopped at his car and pivoted on his heel, turning to face Lemon and Mei. "I promise you. I'm going to figure this out.

****

"They said you wanted to see me?" Lemon's heart wedged firmly in her throat.

Detective Zahn smiled. "Yes. Sorry to bother you again." He held his arm out toward the open door.

Lemon stayed still. "Should I call Andy?"

"No. I promise. I just want to help." Detective Zahn wiggled his fingers. "You can tell him everything we discuss afterward, and I doubt he'll even raise an eyebrow."

Zahn made it all sound very black and white, but Lemon's internal war was not so clear. She was pretty sure Andy was going to be pissed when he found out she talked to the detective without him. But her drive to be polite meshed with her people-pleasing tendencies, and she walked through the doorway anyway.

Once they were alone, Detective Zahn directed her to a cushy chair perched on the edge of a shiny wooden table. The opulent surroundings prompted her to examine the room more closely. It was nice, well-appointed with freshly painted walls and framed prints hanging perfectly on nails.

"This doesn't look like the interview rooms I've been in before."

"That's because it's not an interview room." Zahn slid a water bottle over the smooth surface as he lowered himself into a chair opposite her. "It's a conference room. I told you, this isn't an interrogation."

Lemon twisted the top on the water bottle. The satisfying sound of the plastic teeth breaking loose on the seal hit her ears. "I don't know what else I can tell you. After the other day. I swear I told you everything."

"And I believe you."

"Um, okay." Lemon took a swig of water then instantly regretted it. She stared at the lip. "Is this like a DNA trick?"

Detective Zahn laughed. "First, I think you watch too much true crime. Second, why would that be an issue?"

"I mean, it wouldn't be," she said quickly. "Because I didn't kill anyone."

Amusement danced in the detective's eyes. "Of course you didn't."

Lemon set the bottle on the table and slowly turned it in a circle. "Then what can I do for you?"

"I know you are working with Jade's lawyer. And I think that's fine. I mean, honestly, your dog gets you into enough dangerous places. Then you end up with an ex-girlfriend as a suspect. It's not like you needed to be more enmeshed in another murder case. But," he shrugged. "Apparently, that's your destiny."

Lemon swallowed hard. "It's not by design, believe me."

Detective Zahn chuckled. "Oh, I do. Okay. So, here's what I want to know. Do you have a list of suspects?"

"Me? Me personally?"

"Yeah. I'm asking you. You aren't a lawyer. You aren't a suspect. You are just a person who accidentally ends up in the middle of my cases. And I'm asking you. Who do you think killed Berkely? Or Galen? Or both?"

"Do you think it's the same person?" Lemon asked.

"I'm sorry. I really can't tell you that. Though I guess my chief told you what she thinks during the press release."

"I don't think Jade killed anyone. Or her mom."

Detective Zhan smiled. "I kind of figured. So do you have anyone else in mind?"

"Well, as you know, I saw a man at the dog park. So it might come as a surprise to you that I suspect a woman."

"Hmmm. Interesting. And who is that?"

Lemon twisted her fingers in her lap. "Tammy Ryder."

Detective Zahn leaned forward. "Interesting. Can you tell me why?"

"I don't have much right now. But she's connected to Galen, Berkeley, and Jade's partner in business, Tony. Plus, she's the one that identified Jade's ID as fake. But Jade doesn't know why. She swears that the ID she had with her should be the real one. And I believe her."

"I hear you, Lemon. I do. But we've proven that the ID found with the body is the original one and the one Jade had on her that day was a replica."

Lemon folded her arms over her chest. "Well, then someone stole the real one from Jade's locker and replaced it with the replica without Jade ever knowing."

"I agree."

Shocked by this admission, Lemon's jaw dropped open, and she could do nothing more than stare at Detective Zahn.

"So, you think Tammy did all this? Killed Berkeley and Galen and framed Jade and her mom for it? Why? What's her motive?"

It took Lemon a long moment to answer. "I don't have the motive figured out yet."

"I see." Zahn said. "That's always the hard part. And I find it the most compelling when I investigate the case. I don't really care that the D.A. doesn't have to prove motive in a court of law. I think everyone, a jury included, always wants to know the why. Don't you agree?"

"Yeah."

"So, I guess I need to try to figure out if Tammy has a why." Detective Zahn stood. "And if you come up with one. Let me know, okay?"

Lemon stood as well. "Of course, I will." She shook Detective Zahn's outstretched hand. "I promise."

The detective ushered Lemon out of the room and back into the long hallway at the rear of the police station. Unlike the more public areas of the building, back here there were only uniformed officers and the occasional well-dressed detective, like Zahn, moving up and down the corridor.

Lemon glanced casually at the people they passed, but when a man came toward them, her gaze stuck to him. Just like the last time she'd set eyes on him, his clothing caught her attention first. Beside her, Zahn wore a respectable suit. It probably cost less than two hundred dollars and came off a rack. But the man headed their way wore an expensive, custom-made suit. It was apparent immediately that he was of a different caliber than those around him.

It was just like it had been at the dog park. Except this time, Lemon pulled her focus to his face and kept it there. The thin mustache, trim eyebrows, and steely gaze struck her in the gut. This was the man.

Lemon stopped. Detective Zahn took a few more steps before he turned around. He walked back to stand directly in front of her. "Lemon?"

The man passed them. Just as he was directly beside Lemon, he turned his head to look at her for the briefest of moments. A shiver ran down her spine, bouncing through her until after the man had passed and continued on his way.

"Lemon?"

She focused on the detective, his furrowed brow, his downturned lips. "Can we talk, somewhere private?"

"Okay." Detective Zahn moved, his hand guiding Lemon by her elbow, back to the conference room they'd just vacated. He closed the door, but didn't bother with getting them both seated around the table. "What's going on?"

"That man we just passed in the hallway."

"Yes. What was it about him that got you so jumpy?"

"I saw him at the dog park. That's the guy I saw talking to Galen before he left and ended up dead."

Zahn dropped into one of the seats. "I see."

Lemon pulled a chair away from the glossy table and sat as well, facing the detective. "Who is he?"

"That's Milford Crane."

"The county prosecutor?"

"Yep."

"So, he could be the killer?"

"No. I'm sure he's not. But he didn't mention that he saw Galen that day when I spoke to him." Zahn glanced up at her and flinched as if he just realized he's spoken that part aloud. "It's not a problem. I'll talk to him."

"I mean, it's fishy though, right?"

"No, Galen was a private investigator. He's been known to do con-

tract work for the department. I'm sure their conversation was just business." He sat up straight. "I appreciate you telling me."

"You said to tell you anything."

"I did." He smiled. "Now, I need to get to work. And you, Lemon
Lister, probably have dogs to walk."

Chapter Twelve

Andy plopped onto the couch. Milo immediately tucked himself between his feet. He bent over slowly, as if it took all of his energy to reach down and scratch behind the dog's massive, floppy ears. "Sorry it's so late."

Mei sat down in the recliner. "You look tired, Uncle."

Lemon set a steaming cup of tea on the coffee table in front of Andy before sitting beside him on the couch. "Long day?"

"Yes. Very. But, I heard from Jacob."

Mei shuffled in her chair. "The kid from the pawn shop?"

"Yeah." Andy didn't say anything else, instead he lost himself in stroking Milo.

Lemon wanted to be frustrated by Andy's distraction, but she'd been there. Milo's silky ears were pretty irresistible.

"And? What did he say?" Mei asked.

Andy finally ripped his eyes away from Milo and met her gaze with his own, exhausted one. "He was almost useless. He literally couldn't even tell me the gender of the officer that came by. Only that they were in uniform."

"Wait. Really?"

"Yup. Said he figured they were non-binary. Which is fine. But if that's the case, a description would at least be nice. But good old Jacob had nothing. Said he barely looked at them."

Lemon grasped onto the one part of Andy's statement that gave her hope. "What's the almost helpful part?"

"He said he was distracted because he was fighting with his girl-friend over text. Apparently, he thinks she's been cheating on him with a dude named Kit."

Mei tipped her head. "Okay, but what does that have to do with the cop that came by?"

"Well, it means that he was distracted enough that the officer, or the person impersonating an officer, could easily have taken the necklace without Jacob having a clue about it."

Mei sighed. "But how do we go about finding the thief, who is obviously then also the killer. And potentially Jade's framer?"

Andy chuckled and held up his hand. "One step at a time, sweetie. I need the reasonable doubt to keep Marla Milan out of jail. I have that. I hope. Clearing her, or at least getting her off the top of the suspect list, will make room for the detectives to squeeze another person up there, maybe one with a history of impersonating a police officer."

"I take it you told Detective Zahn all this already then?" Mei asked.

"Just left there."

Lemon cleared her throat. "Did he tell you I was there earlier today, talking to him?"

"Yeah. He said it was an uneventful conversation. Is that true?"

"Not exactly."

Andy straightened his spine. "Okay. Tell me more."

"I mean, it was. Uneventful. At first. I even asked if I should call you. But he said no."

Lemon waited for some response, but got none. So she went on. "But on thc way out we saw the man from the dog park."

"Wait. What?" Mei said. "In the police station?"

"Yeah."

"Like being arrested?" Mei asked.

"No. We weren't in that part of the station. This was in the back. You know." She glanced at Andy. He nodded, the solemn expression on his face stuck as if it were carved of stone.

"Anyway, it turns out it was county prosecutor Milford Crane."

With these words, Andy let out a deep breath. It sent him rocketing into the couch as if the air leaving his lungs propelled him backward. "Wow."

"Wait," Mei said. "This guy—the guy who you saw with Galen Ryan just before he died—is a freaking prosecutor?"

"Apparently."

"How did Zahn take it?" Andy asked.

"He was pretty chill, I guess. He said he'd ask Crane about it. Oh! And he let it slip that Milford Crane didn't mention it to him, like when they were talking about Galen or whatever. That seemed like something he wasn't happy he'd let slip."

Andy rubbed his chin. "That's all pretty interesting."

"So the freaking county prosecutor is a murderer?" Mei asked.

Andy slapped a hand on his knee. "I doubt it."

"That's pretty much what Zahn said, too."

"But he might know something," Mei said. "Uncle, what do you know about this guy?"

Andy shrugged. "Not much. He showed up on the scene after I left SF. But we need to find out. Or, I should say. I do. I have the contacts for this. I'll handle it."

"Okay." Lemon was uncertain of her relief about having this taken off her shoulders. Half of her prepared to jump for joy while the curious part of her that seemed to be reignited by this case deeply regretted the loss.

"So what's our assignment?" Mei asked.

Lemon nearly overheated keeping the secret she and Andy held about her own private assignment. She clapped her hands, calling Milo to her. She pulled his big body onto her lap and focused on giving his enormous ears a thorough scratch so she wasn't tempted to give away her covert assignment to spy on Mei's new girlfriend.

"We need more on Tammy Ryder. Anything you can find out."

Mei sighed. "I feel like that's hard to do."

Andy stood, flicking his gaze briefly at Lemon. "Squeeze that stone. See what you can do. There's more there we haven't uncovered. You've got this."

****

"What are we doing here?" Lemon asked. "Is this really where Caroline wanted to meet? And where is she?"

"She's running late, but she says she'll be here soon." Mei pocketed her phone after reading a text and peered across the table at Lemon. "I don't care what Andy says. We need to find out about this Milford Crane person." She took a long sip of a fruity cocktail from a striped paper straw.

"We're at a gay bar packed with men in leather. What does that have to do with Milford Crane?"

Mei smiled. "Because this is one of his favorite spots, and the way I hear it, he never misses out on the Friday night scene."

Lemon ripped her gaze away from a man whose leather covering left literally nothing to the imagination. "Whoa. Who's your source for this?"

Mei's smirk deepened as she leaned down to take another delicate pull on her straw.

"Are you seriously not going to tell me?" Lemon intended to pull the best friends don't keep secrets card, even though she herself had a great big one.

"Of course I am, but not now, because look." Mei tipped her chin toward the front door, a location she'd carefully placed herself within sightline of, while Lemon was stuck staring at the dance floor. No amount of bisexuality was going to make what was happening there affect her libido. But as she whipped around to peer behind her, she watched Milford Crane waltz through the door.

Even here, he wore a suit, as if he'd walked here straight from the office. But the jacket was unbuttoned, the tie gone, and his collar opened. He looked amazing, almost as amazing as the man on his arm.

"I feel like the entire hotness factor in this building went up by like a hundred degrees," Lemon said.

Mei laughed. "I'll take your word for it. Who do you think the guy is?"

Milford Crane turned to gaze at the young, fresh-faced beauty beside him, and the air between them practically sizzled. "I'd guess that's his date."

Mei tugged her phone back out of her pocket and scrolled through it. "Milford's bio doesn't say anything about a partner."

Lemon counted on her fingers. "Well one, the county probably doesn't update the website every time someone hits the third date. And two, they may not be partners, you know."

Mei rested her chin on the heel of her hand. "That's definitely him, huh? The guy from the dog park?"

"Definitely."

"Sure doesn't look like a killer."

"Do they ever?"

Mei shrugged. "Sometimes I guess. But the thing is, a guy like that, with a good reputation, kind of a rising star—or at least that's what the Internet says—a guy like that wouldn't risk everything to murder some-one in broad daylight, especially after they were seen together in a public place by a witness."

The dreadful feeling that she was potentially the only witness to Milford Crane and Galen Ryan's meeting at the dog park that day crept into her belly and sat there like a sack of rocks.

Lemon tracked his movements through the room. He traveled in fits and spurts as he stopped to greet nearly every person he came across, sometimes gesturing to his date with his free hand, sometimes ignoring him completely. "What else does his bio say?"

"He's from a super prominent family in San Francisco. They've been here since like the gold rush and owned real estate and stuff. Blah, blah, blah. He went to law school back east and interned for some fancy-ass federal judge. But then came back home and got the gig as a county prosecutor within like a minute of the plane landing. But he's super ambitious and wants to be D.A. Apparently, every time he talks to the press he brings that up. He's like, oh I convicted a drug dealer, and I wanna be D.A. I managed to get a rapist in jail for a second, and I wanna be D.A. You know, the normal narcissistic stuff."

"And he's out?"

"Oh yeah, it's like part of his PR campaign."

"Hmmm." With little chance of getting caught staring in the crowded bar, Lemon kept her gaze on Milford. And she was right, he never once looked her way. But his companion did. Whether it was the fact that she and Mei were literally the only women in the place or her staring that snagged his attention she wasn't sure. But his dark-eyed gaze pinned to Lemon and didn't move. Even when Milford moved on, his companion occasionally looked back at her.

Lemon was about to explain this visual showdown to Mei when she heard a new female voice pierce the air around them.

"Hey, you made it!" Mei jumped out of her seat to embrace Caroline. Then both women settled back into the booth, with Caroline wedging herself between Lemon and Mei. "Hey, Lemon."

"Hey."

"I hope you don't mind. I dropped Lyka off at your place."

Lemon's heart thumped. She didn't trust the relationship between Lyka and Snickers. She wondered if the panic showed on her face for a split second. "Oh, um, maybe I should go home, then."

"No, don't worry." Caroline put her hand on Lemon's arm. "I

brought one of Lyka's crates over and left him in there. They'll be just fine."

Lemon let out a heavy breath. "Okay. Thanks."

Caroline turned to Mei. "I saw he's here. I told you, didn't I?"

"You were right. And he's got a date."

Caroline squinted her eyes and leaned forward in a move that was the opposite of inconspicuous. "I don't know who that is." Lemon was about to move her gaze to peek at the subjects of their observation when Caroline sat up, grinned, and waved her hand.

Lemon swiveled her head so fast the lights in the club blurred. Terror climbed up her chest and settled in her throat as she watched Milford Crane and his date walking directly toward their table.

She was still paralyzed when Crane grabbed two chairs from another table without asking and slid them into the cramped space opposite her. "Caroline! What the hell are you doing here?"

His eyes scanned each of them quickly. Lemon tried to assess if his gaze lingered longer on her, but she couldn't tell. His partner, however, openly gawked at Lemon.

"We're just stopping in for the drink specials before heading off," Caroline said. "Let me introduce you to everyone."

"Please," Crane's date said. He batted his eyes at Lemon.

"This is my…ya know…latest person." Caroline giggled. "Mei. She works at the De Young."

"Oh wow," Crane said, with no real enthusiasm. "Super interesting."

The date's eyes fluttered. "I fucking love that place."

"And this is Lemon Lister. Great name, right? She's a dog walker."

"No shit!" The date extended his arm over the table, almost knocking over Mei's fancy drink with his elbow. "I'm Stephen Sikes. And I work at the county shelter. We totally need to be friends."

Lemon couldn't suppress her smile. "I agree. I have a few clients that were rescued from your shelter."

His bright, wide smile practically lit up the room. "That's our goal."

"Well, I guess you two are besties already," Caroline said.

Before either she or Stephen could answer, Milford Crane spoke again, his high-pitched voice ringing through the space. "Caroline, I filed for the election today. Are you still game to work on the campaign? Sure could use your help."

"You know I'm in, Milford. We'll all help. Right girls?" Caroline spun her head first to Mei then, after she got a hearty nod, she turned to Lemon. Uncomfortable with the focus, especially from the eyes of the man she'd seen at the dog park with Galen Ryan, Lemon gave one, curt nod.

"It's settled then!" Milford stood. "So happy to see you again. And I'll be seeing you soon." He turned to Stephen, but the man stayed seated.

He tipped his chin up at Milford. "I'll catch up with you in a bit, darling. I'm just going to hang here with the girls for a sec."

Milford Crane didn't look the least bit offended. Instead he kissed his fingers and touched them to Stephen's cheek. "Don't be too long." Then he turned and walked toward a man in full leather who was holding his hand up in the air and bouncing on his toes.

"So," Stephen leaned across the table toward Lemon. "Let's get to know each other."

"You two do that," Mei said. "I want to dance." She stood and grabbed Caroline's hand.

Caroline hesitated, her gaze flitting between Lemon and Stephen. "Um."

"Come on," Mei said. "Please."

Caroline ripped her gaze away from them and looked up at Mei. "Yeah. Okay." She stood, and with a weird backward glance, she followed Mei to the dance floor.

"So, Lemon Lister. Tell me more."

Lemon rested her elbows on the table, suddenly feeling comfortable in her own skin for the first time all night. "You first, Stephen."

He grinned. The action lit up his hazel eyes, their dynamic color visible to Lemon even in the dim light of the club. They shone back at her, reflecting the yellow bulb-shaped chandelier that hung just inches above their heads, hovering over the table and providing them with a small, lit space to exist in a sea of darkness and leather. "Well, let's start with, I'm Pan, and I was drawn to you the minute I walked in here."

"You mean, the minute you walked in here with your date?"

Stephen dropped his chin on the heel of his hand. "I mean, it's not like a monogamous thing. He's fun, but I bet you're fun, too."

"So you two are just casual, then. Or Poly?"

"I'm open to a lot, honey, but no, we're not Poly, or at least he isn't. We're just casual. That man is too focused on his career to give me the attention I need for a long-term thing."

Lemon sensed an opportunity climbing into her lap. Ignoring her own self-confidence issues that made flirting feel like taking an advanced placement test in biochemistry, she stiffened her spine and plunged into the opening Stephen left. "Oh, yeah. What's his deal?"

"Oooh. You don't know the rising star? Don't tell him that. He'll be crushed."

"Bit of a narcissist?"

Stephen rolled his exquisite eyes toward the ceiling. "That might actually be an understatement. And it'd be an insult if he wasn't so damn smart. He'll go far. And I appreciate that about him. But I'm smart enough to know I won't be the man on his arm when he makes it. It will probably be some fresh-faced, just-passed-the-bar, intern to a Supreme Court Justice." He laughed. "But it won't be me."

"I don't think you're giving yourself enough credit, Stephen."

He grinned at her, his eyes traveling from her face to where the table cut off the view of her lower torso and back up again. "And why's that, Lemon Lister?"

"Well, you're hot."

"Touché."

"And I bet you're smart and successful, too."

He chuckled. "You think?"

"Sure. I mean, I'm a dog walker. So don't feel like I won't be impressed by anything."

"I doubt dog walking, or running a business for that matter, is any-where as easy as people think it is."

"It's not. So what do you do?" Lemon mirrored his posture, placing her own chin in her hand and resting her elbow on the table.

"I'm a stripper."

"Well, you definitely make more money than me, guaranteed."

"Probably, for sure, sweetie. But it also makes me unsuitable for a man with serious ambitions. A dog walker on the other hand…"

"Well, I hate to disappoint you, Stephen, because you're super cute. But I kinda got my heart set on this girl."

"Yeah? Tell me about her."

"She's in jail. And your date put her there."

Stephen frowned. He glanced quickly behind his back before turning back to Lemon. "Tell me everything, sweetie. I got you."

Chapter Thirteen

"Seriously. I can't take all four of you." Lemon stared down at four very boopable noses and eight pairs of pathetic eyes. "I mean, you can't all have to go at the same time?"

But they did. And it wasn't as if Lemon didn't regularly walk four to six dogs. But she knew her own three were a handful. Snickers and Klee were both small but energetic. They tended to run ahead of her. Milo was big, slow, and obsessed with every scent that traveled to his nose within a five-mile radius and lagged behind. Now she had to add in Lyka.

She'd never walked Lyka before. But as soon they all got back from the club, Caroline pointed to where she'd left his harness and leash on one of the many hooks beside the front door and told her he was a good boy and not to worry. Then she'd disappeared into Mei's room in a cloud of drunken giggles.

She was a professional, and she knew how to be safe. There was no way she was taking an unknown along with her own dogs on a group walk in the dark. She pulled herself off the couch and made her way toward the door. "Okay. But two at a time."

When she reached the door, Lyka whined, which elevated him to the top of her needs list. She picked up his harness, and just as Caroline promised, he stepped easily into it. She turned to Milo, who stood quietly as she strapped him into his own harness. She picked up the ends of their leashes, one in each hand for safety's sake, and turned toward the door.

A set of tiny paws hit her calf. She turned to look at Snickers. "Sorry buddy. It'll be your turn soon. Give me fifteen minutes."

Snickers seemed to accept her word and sat back, watching closely as she stepped out with Milo and Lyka. In the hallway, the dogs proved their compatibility immediately. Lyka matched Lemon step by step. Lemon stayed at Milo's pace, and the three moved companionably down the hall to the stairs.

It took a while to get down the three flights and reach the fresh air offered outside the building. But the sidewalk held no appeal for either dog. And unlike Snickers and Klee, who would be perfectly happy doing their business in a small circle of sand surrounding a tree planted in the center of the concrete walk, Milo would not.

She crossed the street and headed to the grass and tree-filled reprieve of the Presidio. The dogs both increased the pep in their step, and Lemon sent a little mental thanks to her parents for gifting her this apartment so close to the natural haven that sat in the city.

When they reached the green oasis, Lemon unclipped Milo's leash. It was something she never got used to doing. But as much as Milo got distracted by his olfactory sense, she'd learned that he was terrified of roads and avoided concrete altogether. He also happened to be mildly obsessed with ensuring that he was fed dinner every night and breakfast every morning, which translated to never losing sight of his meal ticket, aka Lemon.

Lyka, on the other hand, was someone else's dog, meaning he needed to stay attached to Lemon at all times, no matter how well trained he was. It was part of her philosophy. She never took chances with the safety of her clients, and that included dogs she wasn't being paid to walk, like Lyka.

Lyka didn't seem to mind being tethered to Lemon while Milo wandered around free. He relieved himself after they reached the grass, but after that seemed content to say by Lemon's side, moseying slowly across the land, following Milo's irrational, meandering pattern.

Inevitably though, Milo caught a scent. Lemon knew this for sure because his tail stopped its slow sway from side to side. It became a straight rod, a beacon.

"Oh crap," she whispered to herself. She tightened her grip on Lyka's leash and flashed her glance toward him, expecting that Lyka would most certainly catch whatever scent Milo was on.

Milo's proclivity for dead things was one thing, Lyka's trained nose, purposely honed to find human cadavers, was another thing altogether. And with no real experience with an actual professional dog, Lemon prepared for anything.

But Lyka did nothing. Absolutely nothing.

Lyka watched Milo snake his way through a set of low bushes. Lemon turned her attention back to Milo, who stopped, tail still pointed at the sky as if he were trying to beckon the International Space Station to his position. Then he started to paw, the evidence being the dirt that shot up in the air behind him.

"Are you at all interested in what he's got there?" she asked Lyka.

Lyka smiled up at her, his tongue dangling from the corner of his mouth.

"Okay, well, let's go see what he's up to." She moved toward Milo. Lyka easily kept up with her, but he made no effort to so much as sniff at the air, something Snickers and Klee would usually do as they approached Milo and his finds.

"Milo, buddy." Exhaustion bled from her voice. Milo turned, pride painted all over his face. Then he stepped aside in an awkward dance, revealing his prize. "Well, isn't that nice." Lemon frowned down at the matted tail of a squirrel who'd climbed its last tree. "Come on, you found his final resting place, let's leave him in peace now."

One bright point about Milo's macabre hobby, he never felt the need to do anything more than find and alert. He didn't munch on his finds or attempt to bring it to Lemon. Thank God for that.

She reconnected Milo to his leash and walked both dogs back to the house. On their journey, she mulled over the differences in how the dogs reacted to that dead squirrel. Perhaps Lyka only alerted to the scent of humans. That would make sense. In fact, it made a lot of sense because Caroline told her that he could find both living and dead humans.

Lemon picked up her step, an idea forming in her head. She managed to wait to execute her plan until she'd given Snickers and Klee both a chance to go out as well. But as soon as she was back, she started her experiment.

Lemon fished a pair of socks out of her hamper, carefully moving them close to her nose for a sniff. Definitely should work. She placed one sock on her bed and dragged the other along the bedspread, down to the floor at the base of the bed, then across the carpet all way down the hall into the living room where she'd asked all the dogs to stay.

Milo started to dance in circles when he saw her and she wondered if her experiment was about to be ruined by his amateur enthusiasm. "Milo, you wanna go in Lyka's crate and check it out?" Lemon kept Lyka busy with a cookie while coaxing Milo into the metal crate with another.

Milo lumbered in after the cookie then turned at her with a look of sheer betrayal as she hooked the lock closed behind him.

As soon as Lyka was done with his cookie, Lemon shoved the sock at him. "Here buddy, sniff this."

Lyka leaned toward the sock, giving it a tentative investigation. Then he looked up at her expectantly. That's when she realized she didn't know his word. She'd arrived at the park after he did all his searching, so she hadn't heard Caroline say his search command. She ran through a list.

"Go…um, check….um, search?" The dog continued to stare at her, waiting for her to pull out that magic word. Damn. What else was there. "Find?"

As soon as the word left her lips, Lyka was up on all fours and moving. He put his nose to the carpet and bobbed and weaved across the surface in front of her. But even though he ran over the sock's path multiple times, he never stopped and moved along it. Instead, he would glance up at Lemon, wait a beat, then put his head back down.

While this went on for a painfully long time, Milo began to cry. The soft whine was the saddest, most pathetic thing to reach her ears, and Lemon couldn't take it anymore. So as she watched Lyka flounder, she reached back and released the latch on the crate.

Milo quickly mugged her hand, getting a good whiff of the stock still crumpled up in her fist, before taking off. He followed the exact path Lemon had taken, even making a wonky arch in the hallway as Lemon and Lyka followed behind. Milo heaved himself up onto the bed and stood proudly in front of the second sock.

"Okay, so that didn't go as planned." Lemon looked down at Lyka. "Is it because it's my scent?" she asked him. "I mean, that would be confusing, I suppose." She glanced back at Milo who seemed to defy that logic. But nevertheless, she was obviously missing something. "Okay, new experiment. Let's go back to the living room boys."

This time, Snickers and Klee, roused from their post-walk nap by all the commotion, followed Lemon into the bathroom to watch. But Lyka and Milo obeyed her command to stay, so she didn't mind the audience. She pulled a sock out of the mesh hamper only Mei used, then she tipped the hamper on its side so that scent of Mei was fully accessible.

Repeating the process of running the sock through a pathway must have looked comical to Snickers and Klee, both of whom trailed behind her, tails wagging and tongues lolling.

Since the bathroom was closer to the living room, she swooped into the kitchen before heading back to the dogs, making the trail a little less straight-forward, but still not overly difficult.

She didn't bother locking up Milo this time. She presented the sock to Lyka and said, "Find." He began to sniff at the carpet, presumably trying to pick up the trail.

Milo patiently waited until Lyka was over by the television, alternating between sniffing around and glancing up at Lemon, before he took his turn. As soon as he got the scent, he took off.

Lemon stood there in the middle of the living room. To one side of her, Lyka struggled to find anything at all, while Milo's movements traced a perfect map of her footsteps. He disappeared as he looped into the kitchen, then reappeared before sliding out of sight again into the bathroom where the sock trail began.

"Well, Lyka. Something is definitely amiss," she told the dog. He smiled up at her and licked his lips.

****

Mei's crepes were a thing of beauty. Lemon must have watched her make them a million times, and she still had no idea how Mei managed to fit so much flavor into a paper-thin crepe capable of rolling itself around any available filling without so much as a crack. Multiple attempts on her part to duplicate the magic always failed.

Caroline was about to get her first taste of Mei's famous breakfast. "I still feel like you should try this," Caroline said, sliding onto the bar-stool beside Lemon with a freshly poured Mimosa in her hand.

Across the island, Mei set down her spatula and hefted her own glass toward Caroline and Lemon before taking a drink of the yellow, bubbly delight.

"No way," Lemon said. "I know my limitations when it comes to Mimosas."

"No fun, but okay." Caroline winked at her and took a big gulp of her drink, letting out a loud "ahhh" at the end.

"You ladies have fun last night? Or did you just pass out?" Lemon could feel heat in her cheeks as she asked the question.

Mei snickered. "We didn't pass out right away."

"How was Lyka?" Caroline asked. "Did he give you any trouble?"

"Oh, he was great. I took him out with Milo, and they did great together. He is very well behaved."

Caroline glanced over to where Lyka lay, his eyes closed, his chest slowly rising up and down. "He's a good boy. Very well trained. I spent a lot of time training him."

"So, you trained him yourself?" Lemon asked. Caroline whipped her head around so fast it made Lemon back pedal. "I mean, I guess I don't know how all that works, you know?"

Caroline's expression visibly softened. "Oh yeah, sure. I guess I could see how that would be the impression. Some police dogs are trained by other people and then given over to a handler. But I am a certified trainer myself. So I trained Lyka since he was a puppy. I was an officer first, then I trained him and became a K9 officer."

"I think it sounds amazing to be able to train dogs."

Caroline smiled, a dimple popping up in her left cheek. "It's pretty interesting."

"I mean, I work with dogs every day, but I don't know the first thing about training them. I'm super interested in learning about it."

"I have been saying this forever." Mei slid a crepe off the pan, twisted the nob to turn off the burner and walked toward the island with an overflowing plate of crepes in one hand. "You totally need to learn to train those unruly beasts. Not only would it make it easier for you to walk them, but you could make some extra money training people's dogs not to be assholes." She set the crepes on the island beside the bowls of fillings before moving around to drop onto the barstool on the other side of Caroline. "And as I recall, you promised to teach her a couple days ago."

Caroline laughed and batted her eyes at Mei. "I have no idea why I like you. You hate dogs."

Mei flipped a swath of hair. "Hate is strong word. But they're definitely not my favorite. Doesn't matter though. You can't help but like me."

"True." Caroline gave Mei a quick kiss before turning to slide a crepe onto her plate. "You really want to learn to train dogs?" she asked

Lemon.

"Yeah, I mean in general, but also specifically Milo."

"Milo?" Caroline glanced over the hound. "He's pretty chill. I'd think you'd want to start with Snickers."

Despite the fact that Snickers was currently bouncing on her toes trying to beg for a piece of Lemon's yummy breakfast, she was affronted at the attack on her first dog's behalf. And a little annoyed that Caroline had completely forgotten their conversation from a couple days ago. "No sniffing."

Caroline's expression shifted. "Oh, right."

"Oh my god, please!" Mei said. "If that dog digs up one more dead mouse, I am going to puke all over him."

"Yeah, as you know, he likes dead things." Lemon's face heated. Bringing up how Milo bested Lyka at the park when they were looking for Berkeley might not serve her purposes well. She'd gotten the distinct impression that day that Caroline hated the entire situation, so she danced around the subject. But if she was going to get Caroline to demonstrate how she trained Lyka, Lemon had no choice but to tread into dangerous waters.

Caroline looked up from her plate. "So what's the goal here, exactly?"

"Well, if I could find a way to harness his enthusiasm for scent detection in a more productive way, that would be great."

"Less gross," Mei said. "A less gross way."

"Hmm." Caroline turned toward her plate, smearing cream cheese on her crepe. "So what do you want him to find?"

"For starters, I was wondering what exactly is Lyka trained to find?"

"A specific person's scent," Caroline said. "He's not a cadaver dog. That's why Milo was able to find Berkeley and not Lyka. Lyka doesn't look for the scent of death. He seeks out a specific person's scent."

"So, like, I could train Milo to find Mei when she wanders off in the grocery store?"

"This comment seemed to lighten Caroline's mood. "I suppose that would be handy. Girl gets distracted."

"So much."

"Hush it up, both of you," Mei said.

Caroline reached for the raspberry sauce. "I will say that his breed is known for their noses."

Lemon knew that was an understatement of epic proportions. Bassets were second only to Blood Hounds in their ability to detect scents. But she didn't pull out her AKC research card, instead she responded amiably as if Caroline had just dropped a bit of wisdom on her. "He certainly seems interested in smells."

With her crepe fully rolled and drizzled in deep red sauce, Caroline held her fork above it and turned to glance at Lemon. "So you want me to help you train him?"

"Please?" Lemon asked.

"Say yes," Mei said.

"Okay. I'll do it."

Chapter Fourteen

Lemon hated this room just as much now as she did on her first visit. The drab walls, concrete floor, and sharp florescent lights had not improved an ounce. Even the creepy, crawly sensation floating in her stomach as the guard's hawk-like eyes watched her, remained the same.

At her side, Andy focused on his tablet, scrolling through something Lemon didn't bother to peek over his shoulder to see. Lemon concentrated on her breath as she watched the door. In and out. In and out.

The door opened, revealing Jade in her drab jail gear, her hair slung into a messy bun on top of her head. Her eyes, rimmed in red and perched on top of purple bags were just as beautiful as ever as they shone when they caught sight of Lemon.

Lemon couldn't help but stand, her body instinctively drawn to Jade. But the officer hanging onto Jade's elbow mouthed no, a quiet reminder of the rules of this miserable situation. Lemon tracked Jade's movements, dropping back into her own seat at the same time Jade fell into hers.

"Jade, how are you doing?" Andy asked.

She smiled at him. "Better now. Thanks for getting me moved."

Clueless as to what they were talking about, Lemon turned to Andy. But he was back to staring at his tablet again.

"Was something wrong?" Lemon asked.

Jade sighed. She looked exhausted. "It was my roommate…uh, cellmate. She found out I worked in law enforcement and, well Andy fixed it. It's all good."

"You tell me if anything changes, right away," Andy said, looking up at her.

"I promise."

"Listen Jade, we came here to ask you something very specific."

"We did?" Lemon asked.

Andy chuckled. Lemon glanced at Jade, who actually flashed a half smile. "Andy does that 'need to know thing' doesn't he?"

Lemon stared at the side of Andy's face. "Yeah, he does. I thought we were just coming to see you."

"You're here so Jade can have a friendly face. I have an agenda."

Jade's slight smile grew wider. The sight was like a glass of warm milk for Lemon's soul. Andy let them have a moment.

Eventually Jade's lips fell, and she turned back to Andy. Lemon wondered if they were thinking the same thing, that this moment was as sad as it was nice. Because Lemon would walk out of here alone, and Jade would stay.

"So, Andy, tell me," Jade said.

Andy set his tablet down and folded his hands together. "What do you know about Milford Crane?"

"The prosecutor angling for the D.A. job?"

"The very one."

Jade dropped her hands on the table, the clink of the metal handcuffs against the tabletop sending a shock of alarm along Lemon's spine. "Same as most people, I guess. He's got a great record that matches his ambitions."

Andy leaned over, his forearms planted firmly on the table. "What if I told you I heard a rumor that some people think Crane plants evidence in order to get convictions."

"I'd say that's unlikely."

"And why's that?"

"Even if he had dirty cops to do that for him, all that evidence goes through the crime lab. He'd have to have an ally at the lab. And more than that. Everything is double and triple checked. We have a lot of protocols in place."

"So, there's no way to plant or fake evidence and have it go through the lab?"

One of Jade's cheeks popped inward as if she were biting it. Her eyes closed for a moment. Lemon had seen this expression before. Jade deep in thought was a thing of beauty. "It could be done. But Tammy would have to be in on it. There's no way it could happen under her nose without her knowing."

"So, if the rumor were true, a few people would have to be involved, and one of those people would certainly have to be Tammy, yeah?"

"A few weeks ago, I would've laughed at the possibility. But now…I don't know anymore. Something is really, really wrong. Berkeley is dead—murdered—and I've been framed. Even my mom got dragged into this."

"Which begs the question, is it possible you know something that you don't know you know? Something that makes you a threat?"

"Believe me, Andy, I've been dragging through my brain every second of the day. And I just can't think of anything. All I've got is that Berkeley must have known something, and it got her killed. I just happened to be an easy target for framing."

"I think so, too. So next question, is there any chance Berkeley gave you any hints as to what she knew?"

"The thing is," Jade's eyes flashed to Lemon and back to Andy, "we just started really talking again a few weeks before she went missing. It wasn't that we hadn't stayed friends after we broke up or anything like that. We did. But we didn't talk that much. It was just, you know, like the occasional text or whatever. But we didn't see each other often. I think we ran into her at a club once." Jade met Lemon's gaze and held it, asking for confirmation.

"Yeah. I remember. That was the first, and only time, I ever met her."

"It was congenial?"

"Oh yeah, for sure," Lemon said. "She was nice."

"She was very nice. We didn't make it as a couple because she never told me what upset her, and then it all built up into a big fight." Jade's gaze stayed on Andy as if she were purposely ignoring the elephant in the room that was her and Lemon's own relationship issues. "Anyway, she was a good person."

"Moral, ethical?"

Jade's head jerked back as if she'd been struck. "What are you asking?"

"The obvious. Is there any way Berkeley was caught up in Milford's scheme to plant evidence, if there was in fact a scheme, that is?"

"No way. Not Berkeley."

"Okay. So back to the weeks before she went missing. You were talking pretty regularly, right?"

"Mostly texting, yeah. She was in a new relationship and it was rocky right from the start. And I was…Lemon and I were on a break."

Lemon's stomach quivered. Of all the things she regretted lately, hurting Jade was at the top of her list, especially over something that seemed so trivial now.

"Do you know who she was seeing?"

"She never called her by name. A fellow cop I think though. At least that's the impression I got."

"Anything stand out about those conversations? Or anything she said about the new girlfriend? Anything at all?"

A tear escaped Jade's left eye. "I'm sorry, Andy. I really am. I wish I could remember something. But it was just the usual. Giving each other sympathy, talking to each other. Giving advice. That kind of thing."

"Okay. Let's try something else. What did she say that made you think the love interest was also a police officer?"

"I'm not sure if it was anything in particular. It was more like she made it sound as if she saw this person in the course of her daily work life, you know. Like one time it was around lunch time, and we were going to meet up for a bite. But she said this person—she called her the cute girl, not her girlfriend—like they weren't that serious yet. Anyway, she said the cute girl was on a call with her partner and needed Berkeley's help."

"So that definitely sounds like this person is a cop then."

"Yeah. That's what I figured."

"Never a name?"

"Sorry. No."

"Any chance their relationship was violent?"

Jade shivered, her skin visibly moving before Lemon's eyes. "I hope not. I mean. There wasn't any hint that was the case. Do you think Detective Zahn knows about this person?"

"Not sure. He's keeping things close to the vest, just as we'd expect him to. But I'll mentioned it to him, for sure."

The door to their tiny room flew open startling the two officers standing on either side of it. A man in uniform stormed in. "Andy Hall?"

"Yes?"

"There's an urgent call for you from Detective Zahn."

"Well, speak of the devil."

****

The trip from the county jail to the police station was a blur. Lemon rode in the passenger side of Andy's car, clutching her hands together in her lap. Andy seemed disturbingly calm. He didn't so much as break the speed limit as he navigated his way along the crooked two-mile path from the county jail to SFPD headquarters.

They didn't speak during that short ride. Instead, Andy kept a laser focus on the road. Lemon alternated between watching Andy and staring out the windshield as they moved through the Mission Bay neighborhood.

So many people strolled along the sidewalks, hurried across streets, or stood at bus stops, their heads curved over their phones. None of them rode beside a lawyer on a journey of unknown purposes between the jail their girlfriend—or ex-friend, or kind-of girlfriend—was being held to the police station to meet up with a homicide detective.

The walk into the station from the parking lot chilled Lemon to the bone. The sun ducked behind thick grey clouds, leaving the city at the whim of the cool wind drifting off the Bay. As soon as they hit the lobby, an officer approached them, as if she'd actually been waiting. Why was this little visit so important? Was someone else dead?

This dreadful thought struck Lemon at the exact moment the officer opened their mouth. "Mr. Hall?"

"Yes."

The officer's eyes flicked to Lemon, but they said nothing to her. Instead, they spun on their heel and swung their hand in an arc. "Please follow me."

They didn't head into the back area of the station this time. Instead, they went down the wide, linoleum-lined hallway to one of the interview rooms. Lemon glanced at Andy for a sign of alarm, but his cool, calm demeanor held. He pulled a metal chair out for Lemon before dropping into the one beside her.

Two matching chairs stared back at them, empty and waiting, from across the table. Lemon couldn't take it anymore. "Andy, what the hell is going on?"

Andy turned his head and flashed her a small smile. "I don't know Lemon, but it'll be okay. Let's just wait and see what the detective has to say."

Apparently, her anxiety projected from her very skin. Lemon shook out her shoulders and rolled her neck in an attempt to loosen some of the tight muscles squeezing at her. All that work collapsed when Detective Zahn marched into the room and quickly sat in one of the chairs opposite them, dropping a thick, manila folder on the table beside his space.

"Thanks so much for coming over on short notice. I do, however, need to speak to you alone, Mr. Hall."

Andy's voice was cooler than Lemon had ever heard it. "Is there a reason my employee can't stay? If there is, and she's a suspect, I'd definitely like to be open about that. As I will also serve as her counsel."

Before she had the chance to fully panic about her own potential arrest,

Zahn held up his hand. "No. Absolutely not." He glanced over at Lemon. "That's definitely not the case. I just didn't realize she was an employee. Okay, let me just get to the point." Zahn took a deep breath. "We found an email someone tried to delete."

Andy leaned over the table, his forearms planted on the wood. "I'm listening."

"The email was from Galen Ryan, sent exactly two hours and fourteen minutes before he was murdered."

Lemon felt the hinge of her jaw as it dropped.

Andy, completely unfazed, asked, "What did it say?"

Zahn cleared his throat, clearly uncomfortable. "The email implicates Prosecutor Crane in some nefarious dealings."

"What kind of dealings?" Andy asked.

"Well, I'm not real inclined to give details at this exact moment."

"Then why am I here?"

"Because he's in another interview room right now, and he's asking for a lawyer. You specifically."

Andy barked out a laugh. "Is that right?"

"He says you're the best."

"Well, he's right about that." Andy stood suddenly, shocking Lemon, who fumbled to shove her own chair away from the table. "But I'm not representing Milford."

Zahn stood as well, staring across the room at Andy. "May I ask why?"

"Because I've known Milford Crane since he was in middle school.

He's never been anything but an entitled brat. And I'm retired."

Zahn chuckled. "You're not very good at being retired, Andy."

"Not when it comes to defending innocent people, no. Is that all? Or do you want to tell me something that will exonerate my client?"

"Nope. Nothing else I can reveal today."

"Well, we've got to get back to our client."

Zahn scratched the top of his head. "Okay. Thanks for coming down."

"Sure thing. Let's go, Lemon."

Five minutes later, Lemon sat in Andy's car, watching as he snapped his seatbelt into place. "Andy?"

He looked up at her and sighed. "I do not like that man. Crane, not Zahn. I've known his dad for many years, we served in the prosecutor's office together. He was alright, but there was always an edge to the guy I just didn't trust, you know what I mean?"

Lemon shrugged. She'd dog sat for a cold-blooded killer and didn't know it, so she probably wasn't the best person to talk to about intuition.

"Well, I just never fully trusted him. And his kid is twice as sketchy. If I got an email from one of his contractors saying he was doing bad shit, I would believe it like that." Andy snapped his fingers. "The truth is, when I really stop to think about it, I wouldn't put it past Crane to kill someone to keep his secrets."

Lemon sucked in a breath. "You think he might have killed Galen?"

Andy hit the button to start the car. "I'm beginning to think it's a possibility. And more important, I think Zahn does, too."

Lemon ran her tongue along the roof of her mouth, finding it dry and sour. "Do you think he could have killed Berkely, too?"

"It's certainly a possibility. No matter what, though. I promise you. I will find out."

Chapter Fifteen

Caroline squared her shoulders. "Okay, watch closely."

Lemon had her sights trained on Caroline and Lyka, every molecule of her being focused on the pair. Nothing got by Lemon's intense gaze. But she didn't vocalize that. She just nodded.

"Lyka sniff."

The dog pressed his nose to the piece of fabric Caroline held in her hand. Lemon listened for the accompanying sniffing sound. She'd become accustomed to it. Milo's was loud. Snicker's was soft and meek, and Klee's lie somewhere in between, a middle-ground noise that Lemon registered easily.

But Lyka's sniff must have been so subtle and quiet that Lemon couldn't hear it at all. Because after pressing his nose to the fabric, he looked up at his person. Caroline made a quick gesture with her hand, and Lyka immediately jumped into action.

The dog took off, nose to the ground, just like Milo did when he was stuck on a scent. Lyka's long, graceful legs propelled his slim body forward, in deep contrast to Milo's enthusiastic waddling. Lyka's route was meandering, he bobbed in big arcs and swoops. This also stood in contrast to Milo's more slightly drunken but otherwise straight-line technique.

Lyka made his way to the dark, green bush where Caroline had hidden the matching piece of fabric, both sprayed with an identical scent. He stopped at the bush and sat, staring over at his handler.

Caroline made a hand gesture. It happened in a flash, but Lemon thought she saw her finger and thumb form a circle. Lyka popped up and ran to her to receive a treat. "Good boy." Caroline patted his head.

"So, can you explain all the hand gestures?" Lemon asked.

"I can. But every dog and their handler have their own commands. I mean, you can make them what you want. But basically, I have four commands in the search." Caroline paused in her explanation to tell Lyka to lie down. The dog sprawled at her feet and dropped his head between his paws.

Once Lyka was relaxed, his eyes drooping toward a quick nap,

Caroline turned back to Lemon. "So there's sniff, which can be a verbal command, or a hand gesture." Caroline touched her finger to her nose. "That's the signal that I want him to get this particular scent. If we're tracking a person, he will pick up that scent. If we're looking for a cadaver, I'll use a scent jar that has…well, you can guess."

"Which scent did you use when you were looking for Berkely?" Lemon asked, her mind drifting back to Lyka's unsuccessful outing that day.

Caroline pressed her lips together, a look of sheer annoyance draping her features. "Well, I did it wrong that day. I used the gun as the scent. I should have used a piece of fabric with Berkeley's scent. See, I think he was looking for the last person to touch that gun, which easily could have been the killer, not Berkeley."

"But I heard they didn't find fingerprints on the gun. So, if it was wiped clean, or the killer used a glove, how would their scent be on it."

"The dog is better than fingerprints. Their nose is so much more powerful than we can image. If the killer put the gun on their person while they carried it, say in a pocket or waistband, it would retain their scent, no matter how much wiping they did. And if they wiped it with a cloth that they had touched, forget about it."

Lemon's mind wandered back to that fateful day at the park. Berkeley and Lyka stood by the abandoned gun, with a dissatisfied Detective Zahn at their side. Milo took one sniff of that gun and took off. He'd traveled nearly half a mile from their starting place to Berkeley's final resting place among the trees. But what Lemon still didn't know was what, exactly, Milo was tracking. Was the scent of Berkley from the gun, or the scent of the killer, having deposited Berkeley in the bushes then carrying the gun to where it was discarded? Or had Milo detected the sweet of smell of death, his personal favorite, from the gun to the woman? Lemon just didn't know. And Milo wasn't talking.

"So, how do you figure that out?" Lemon asked. "I mean, what if the cops needed to know if the scent is from the owner or the person who carried it afterward?"

Caroline smiled brightly. "That's easy. You do a control experiment. Just like we did, with planted scents. Let's do another one." Caroline moved toward the bush and piece of fabric nestled between its rich green leaves.

"Can I plant the scent?"

Caroline ignored this request. "The second command is to follow the scent. That's when he begins to track. Then after he indicates he's found the highest concentration of the scent, he signals, that was the sit, I give a command to come back to me and get a treat."

"So that's three commands. What is the fourth?"

"Oh. That's only used if he gets distracted. I have a command for him to refocus. That's an important part of the training."

"Can you show me?"

"Maybe. We'll try again and see if he gets distracted. You can even distract him if you want to."

"Okay. Can I plant the scent this time?"

Caroline ignored the request again, and moved quickly. She grabbed the fabric and jogged toward another set of thick vegetation. She wedged it between two fluffy Hydrangeas and made her way back to where she'd left Lyka sitting calmly at Lemon's feet, his leash gripped in her hand.

Caroline took the leash from Lemon. "Lyka, sniff." The exact same set of actions played out once again. The dog touched the cloth with his nose, then turned at Caroline's hand signal and wove a long and circuitous route that eventually ended at the scent jar. But Lemon was on high alert this time. She noticed the way the dog picked up his nose just before each snake-like turn of his body. He made eye contact with Caroline briefly before ducking back down and continuing on the path. The dog did this four times between sniffing the fabric and finding the jar.

Something about this wasn't right, but Lemon couldn't determine exactly what was happening, she wasn't qualified for that. But she knew someone who was. Someone who also knew Detective Zahn. So as she watched Lyka receive pets, praise and a handful of cookies for finding his prize, Lemon formulated a plan.

****

"Oh baby, I know you're going to miss Mommy, but you're in good hands." Caroline patted Lyka's head before grabbing the door handle.

"The best hands," Mei said. "Come on. Let's get to the restaurant."

Lemon smiled at them both and waved. "You have about seventy minutes to get to the restaurant and eat before the show. Go!"

"What would I do without my personal planner," Mei smiled at her and chucked her chin before ducking out the door Caroline held open for her.

"Have fun."

Once the door was closed, Lemon whirled on her heel to face the crowd. Her own three dogs were splayed out on their respective beds. Snickers, chin resting on two fluffy paws, looked up at her. Klee rolled over on his back and pawed at the air. Milo snorted. His eyes drooped shut, so it could have actually been a snore.

"We're gonna go. Be good, kay?"

With the exception of Snickers licking his lips, she got no reaction. "Fine. Forget them. Let's go, Lyka." Lemon picked up his harness. The dog obediently sat and let her put it on him. She quickly latched the harness and stood up, glancing at the digital time glowing back at her from the microwave.

She cursed. Shoving Mei and Caroline out the door had taken even longer than she expected. Now she and Lyka were going to be late. She shut the door of the apartment and sped down the stairs, stopping at the building entrance to peek out of the diamond glass set in the old wooden, Victorian door. She watched as Caroline's car pulled away from the curb, counted to twenty, and bolted outside.

It didn't take her long to get to the small patch of ground in the Presidio where she'd set the meeting place. Lyka was a much quicker walking companion than Milo.

When they arrived, Christina stood beside a small, concrete bench. A Kelly green backpack perched on the bench, its zipper opened and a gaping hole staring up at the sky. "Hey, you made it." Christina smiled, the action pushing round sunglasses up her nose.

"So sorry we're late! It took me forever to get his handler out the door."

Christina frowned. "I am not a fan of testing a dog behind their handler's back."

Lemon came to a stop in front of Christina. Lyka sat politely at her side. "I know, and I'm really sorry about the deception. I am. But if this dog is tracking evidence," she pointed at the regal Shepard, "And he can't…ya know…actually do it…"

Christina held up her hand. "I understand. It's just a little grey area. I'm not big on grey areas. But after Detective Zahn called me, I didn't really feel like I had a choice. All this is off-the-record. He was clear about that. My opinion on this dog here today isn't official. If we needed to make it official, I would need to replicate it in front of law enforcement. You understand that?"

"I totally do. Zahn explained the whole thing to me. He said this was like a test run to see if there's even really an issue to worry about."

"Yes. That's my understanding, too." She frowned down at Lyka. "He's a beautiful dog. Very well behaved."

"Oh for sure. He's the best trained dog I've had the pleasure to walk. Most of my clients treat a leash like it's a sled dog tether. He is truly amazing. Super smart. Super well-behaved. Follows commands like that." Lemon snapped her fingers. Lyka instantly dropped to a down position.

"Point demonstrated." Christina squatted down in front of Lyka and looked off into the distance, her hands dangling between her knees lazily. "Do you know his release word?"

"Release word?"

"The word his handler says when she wants to communicate to him that he's free to go. Get up, do his own thing."

"Oh, maybe." Lemon had an amazing memory. It was part of the reason her clients liked her so much. She could always remember every dog's special quirks, diets, commands, likes, etc. She'd definitely heard Caroline use a word when she took Lyka's harness off and let him run loose in the apartment. "Be Free."

As soon as the words left her mouth, Lyka stood. He stretched his back legs and dipped his head, leaning toward Christina. She continued to gaze out toward the top of the Golden Gate bridge which peeked out above the low hanging fog nestled at its base. Lyka took one tentative step and then another. He sniffed at Christina's casually dangling hands for a moment, then sat pretty in front of her. Finally, Christina ripped her gaze away from the view to give her attention to Lyka.

After a petting session complete with low talk and whispers to the dog, Christina stood and reached into her backpack. "I'm going to have you place this in the bushes over there while I distract him, okay?" She handed a small tin jar with a mesh top to Lemon.

Lemon didn't question the instructions. Zahn told her to do whatever Christina asked her to do. And she had no plans to disappoint. She walked to the area Christina pointed to, where a set of low, yellowish-green bushes jutted out into the grassy area. Lemon set the tin just under the lowest branches.

"Perfect," Christina called. "Now walk back to me using the same route."

Lemon did as she asked. When she arrived, Christina stood. "I don't know if this dog is trained to search or track. Do you?"

Lemon shrugged. "I'm sorry. I guess I don't know the difference."

"If he's trained to search, he'll run his nose over the ground until he hits the scent he's looking for. If he's trained to track, he'll follow the track of a scent. The way I imagine your Bassett Hound does."

"Caroline says he can do both."

"On the same command?"

"Yeah. She just says sniff."

Christina's brow furrowed. "Okay, no problem." She smiled. "We'll figure it out ourselves. Let's start with tracking." She led Lyka over to Lemon and pointed at her. "Sniff."

Lyka stuck his nose to Lemon's thigh before dropping it to the ground. He weaved his way along the ground, veering further and further off the trail Lemon had walked. He looked up at Christina several times, but she stayed completely still.

Eventually, the dog looped around in a circle and made his way back to the two women, sitting pretty in front of them, his tongue lolling out of his open mouth.

"Okay," Christina said, her tone giving away nothing. "Let's try a search, shall we." She pulled another tin out of her backpack. This one, identical to the one Lemon hid in the bushes, also had a mesh top. "This has the same scent as the one you hid," she explained.

The dog stuck his nose to the top of the tin as Christina held it in front of him and gave the verbal command. After sniffing it, he moved away from them, nose to the ground. Christina stood and stared at the dog, her bottom lip trapped between her teeth. "That's weird," she said as Lyka floundered wildly across the grass.

"What's weird?"

"I don't think he sniffed at all."

"See, I wondered about that. When Milo sniffs I can hear it, you know. But with him, there's nothing."

Christina tapped her chin with her forefinger. "I wonder…"

Lemon desperately wanted her to finish that statement. But Christina merely dropped to her knees and called Lyka back. She gave him pets and treats before hefting her backpack over her shoulder. "How much time do we have?"

Lemon had only met Christina once, at a dog convention. They'd exchanged cards and talked about how Christina read about Milo's discovery in the papers. She mentioned she knew Detective Zahn, had trained some of his family pets, apparently. Lemon's memory of that distinct moment had led to the collaboration, but she didn't really know the woman, and the more she talked the more of a mystery she became.

With no choice but to ride this train until she found its destination, Lemon told her, "We have a lot of time. Mei and Carline are going to a musical."

"Good. I have a friend we need to go see. She's not too far away. I'll drive."

Lemon moved to keep up with Christina as she loped across the grass with Lyka's leash in her hand. "Where are we going?"

"To see a vet."

Chapter Sixteen

Lemon's chest ached. Holding onto a deep, dark secret was bad enough. Keeping it from her best friend was going to kill her.

"Did you enjoy the show?"

Mei turned away from the stove and glanced over at Lemon. Perched on a barstool at the island, coffee in hand, Lemon smiled back at her.

"It was awesome. I'm sorry I didn't take you, though."

"What? Why?"

Mei shrugged. "I just think you would have liked it. And we used to do things like that together."

"Used to? Mei, we went to the movies last week."

Mei turned back to the crepes she was making. "I know, but, it's weird going without you."

"It's fine. You have a new girlfriend."

Mei's words barely made it over her shoulder to Lemon. "She's not my girlfriend. We're just dating."

The statement felt weird to Lemon, off somehow. Sure, they literally met a week ago at the place where Mei found a gun and Milo found a body, but they seemed pretty serious. "Oh. I mean, I thought it was more than that."

Mei shook her head, but said nothing. Had they fought last night? Caroline and Lyka left early, but she assumed they just went to work. Caroline even brought her uniform over the night before, leaving it hanging on the back of the linen closet door in the hallway, for some bizarre reason.

"Did you talk to Andy last night?" Mei asked.

"No. Why? Was I supposed to?"

"He just texted me asking if we're up." Mei leaned to one side, peering at her phone.

Lemon glanced at the digital clock over the microwave. Did Andy sleep? He came over late and called before seven in the morning. For a person who claimed to be retired, this man was relentless. "Well, we're up. I got dogs to walk in twenty."

Mei twisted the knob on the stove, slid the last crepe out of the pan, and picked up her phone. "Guess we better multi-task then." She handed the phone to Lemon. "You call him, I'll get breakfast."

Lemon took a satisfying sip of her coffee and punched up Andy's cell number. He answered on the second ring. "Ladies! You finally got up."

Mei slid over to the island, a plate stacked with crepes in one hand. "Please, Uncle, it's early as hell."

His deep chuckle echoed through the line. "Whatever you say. Listen, I have some bad news."

No one had ever delivered bad news with such a cheery attitude. Despite the tendrils of anxiety creeping up her spine, Lemon couldn't resist the smile that spread across her lips. "What is it?"

"The D.A. isn't going to press any charges against Milford Crane. In fact, he's not in any trouble at all, and Detective Zahn has been instructed not to interview him again."

"What the fuck?" Mei said. She dropped her forearms on the kitchen island at the same moment that her jaw hinged open. "I mean. The dude is shady as shit. He was working on shady shit with Gaylen *and* Lemon *saw* the dude at the dog park with Galen like minutes before Gaylen ended up dead. What the fuck else does she need?"

"It sounds very good," Andy said. "But it doesn't matter because he has an alibi."

"How can that be?" Lemon asked. "He was definitely there. I saw him."

"I have no idea. Don't have a clue what he's claiming his alibi is, and of course, they aren't telling me."

"Wait. Don't they have to tell you everything? Discovery or whatever?" Mei asked.

" 'Fraid that's a long way off, kiddo. There's a lot more legal steps before we get to that. And I'm hoping I will get Jade released before we hit any of those steps. I'm not really in the mood for a trial. I met an amazing woman the other day. I'm planning to be busy here pretty soon."

"You're ridiculous," Mei said. "Listen, what can we do to blast this guy's alibi out of the water?"

"While I love your enthusiasm, kiddo, it's going to be pretty damn hard to blow up his alibi when we don't know what it is."

"Thanks for letting us know, Andy," Lemon said. "And be sure to contact us if there's anything we can do."

Andy gave them a parting phrase about being good or careful or both and Lemon slammed the red button. "I think we need to find out what the alibi is." The statement was said with conviction even if her action of jumping up from the barstool and grabbing a set of leashes didn't match her intentions. "I don't know how we're gonna to do it. But we will. I gotta walk some dogs. Use your giant brain."

Mei just winked at her from across the island. "On it."

****

There were few places as beautiful in the morning as this little hill. Muffin the Shih Tzu led the pack, her tiny ponytail bouncing on the top of her head as if it were a ranger hat signaling that she knew the way. Behind her a rag tag batch of five, wildly varying dogs, loped happily along the concrete path with Lemon at the back strapped to them all with colorful leashes secured to her waist.

As Muffin crested the hill, the striking shape of the iconic orange bridge spanning across the Golden Gate rose into view. As often happened this time of day, it was partly obscured by the dusty white fog hugging its towers.

This right here explained to anyone who questioned her why Lemon revisited this path behind the Legion of Honor. Afterall, it was the unfortunate site of the devastating discovery of Snicker's original owner's disembodied feet. But despite her willingness to overcome that trauma for the view, she still had never brought Milo here again.

She would have to turn the dogs around soon and get back to the van so she could begin dropping them off. That would leave her about an hour to get lunch and walk her own dogs before heading back out with the mid-day pack.

Despite the nice walk, gorgeous scenery, and well-behaved pups, Lemon was still plagued with all the worries crowding her mind. Her fall-out with Jade before all the current troubles seemed petty and stupid now, creating an ache of regret she couldn't seem to escape. Every night as she lay in her warm, soft bed, three snoring canines at her feet, she stared at the ceiling and wondered what Jade was going through.

That constant dull pain greeted a newer one. The secrets she kept from Mei about her investigation into Lyka's abilities. Her clandestine meetings with Christina the dog trainer, and that trip to the vet.

Christina's face had reflected Lemon's own as they stood with Lyka outside the vet's office. Lemmon couldn't swallow secretly taking someone else's dog to the vet. But Detective Zahn, as he greeted them in the parking lot with another K-9 officer at his side, assured them that Lyka was a working dog. He worked for the police department. Therefore, the K-9 officer, Jambeck was his name, had every right to take Lyka in for an examination.

As she ran over the events of the night before, Lemon turned the pups back around and began to jog toward the van. Perhaps she wanted to give them some more vigorous exercise, or perhaps she was just trying to outrun her own demons. Neither Caroline nor Mei, nor anyone outside the group at the vet's office, knew what she knew or carried what she now carried.

As she neared the intersection of the grassy meadow surrounding the path and the black asphalt of the Legion's parking lot, she slowed, allowing herself the chance to catch her breath and the dogs to get in any last-minute business.

As she watched Noodle the Beagle follow his powerful nose across the tips of the wide blades of grass, she flinched. A dog with a poor sense of smell. It was very sad for sure. But Dr. Jurn didn't seem overly worried about Lyka. She said he could smell enough to keep him from living in the world completely blind, and because she believed he was born this way it wasn't difficult or terrifying for him, as it might be for a dog losing his scent in old age.

Dr. Jurn said a dog's sense of smell was like a human's sight. It was very sharp, and they relied on it to navigate the world. She spent a lot of time making sure he was safe and healthy in every other way. And that meant a lot to Lemon and Christina.

Detective Zahn and Officer Jambeck stood quietly during the exam and the subsequent conversation. But then they peppered Dr. Jurn and Christina with questions. Did this mean Lyka couldn't do the job he was actually doing? Did it mean he never was able to do it? Did it mean all the things he'd found in the past were somehow faked? Would his handler have known, or was it the dog faking it?

This last question made Christina and Dr. Jurn laugh. Neither thought that Lyka was committing some major fraud upon the police department. No, they both agreed, his handler had to have known. And it was she who was committing the fraud.

Lemon did not sleep a wink last night. Only mild relief greeted her when she woke up to find Mei cooking breakfast and Caroline nowhere to be seen. She would have preferred that Mei slept in. Facing her best friend while carrying this secret about the woman she was dating might just end up eating Lemon alive.

The dogs moved slowly across the parking lot toward the van. Lemon ruminated on how Andy saved the day by giving her and Mei a new, and seemingly impossible puzzle to solve. Caught up in her thoughts, she nearly got taken out by a car swooping into the parking spot beside the van.

Lemon checked to make sure she still had six live dogs with her before rounding on the small electric car. It's driver and passenger emerged simultaneously, tumbling out of opposite doors and rushing toward Lemon and her pack.

How Mei ended up in a car with Tony Jillian was a question that might have broken Lemon's brain if she had to dwell on it. Instead, both Tony and Mei leapt in front of her. Mei kept her hands tucked beneath her chin as she peered down warily at the dogs. Tony, however, dropped down to crouch in front of them, accepting kisses and snugs with enthusiasm.

Lemon's speech couldn't seem to keep up with her rapidly whirling mind. "What are you doing here? Together? With each other? Here?"

"I called Tony. You left his number on a sticky note in the kitchen. Listen, he knows Tammy and Gaylen and Milford." Mei's eyes might have been as wide as Lemon's. She felt as though her lashes might pop off from the stretch of her eyelids.

"Yeah. Um. Wow."

Tony glanced up at Lemon from his spot on the ground. "I do, and I have some fucking thoughts about Milford Crane." Tony stood and glanced around wildly. The museum would be open soon. Cars were starting to arrive. Other dog walkers and golfers headed to the course behind the museum were wandering through the area. "Let's go somewhere quiet."

****

Tony Jillian sitting at their kitchen table seemed surreal. His short hair clung to his head where it peeked out beneath his orange ball cap. His jeans-clad legs dropped beneath the barstool with just a touch more length than Lemon's. His expressive hands slid across the countertop as he wove his tale.

"I suppose you know Tammy and Galen were a couple. It was serious, too. They were hardcore for a few years, and then suddenly." He snapped his fingers. "They just split. It happened while I was working at the crime lab. And he used to be there all the time, like at least two or three times a week. Then out of the blue, he quit showing up. I didn't see him for like five or six weeks. Then he shows up, and he fucking wants to talk to me. He never fucking talked to me, right. It was always straight to Tammy's office, even if it was about work."

"Okay, back up," Mei said. "We heard you and Tammy were an item."

Tony scrubbed at his eyes with the back of his hand. "For a minute, yeah. I'm not proud of it. And it wasn't serious. Look. The point is, she was still totally into Galen. That's why we didn't work. And proof was in the fucking pudding. The guy kept coming around even after she and I were together."

"But supposedly he was there for work right? So why was he there all the time for work? He's like a private eye or something, right?"

"No. He's a contractor. He does different jobs, usually for law enforcement. Usually for Milford Crane. It seemed like for a while there Milford was the only person he was doing work for at all."

"What kind of work, exactly?" Mei asked.

Tony scratched his forehead, making his hat bounce up and down. "The detectives are swamped with major crimes. They don't have the time to deal with some of the details they can contract out."

"Is that legal?" Mei asked.

"Sure. If the contractor is doing things that don't require a police officer to do. So like helping with a missing person's search or talking to someone like me after the police release a crime scene, and I pick it up. Or, I don't know, other shit. It's legal. But I think the line is kind of thin."

Lemon looked up from her phone. Surprised by what Tony was saying, she did a little Internet searching. "I guess so."

She showed her phone to Mei who glanced quickly at the list of articles. "Okay, so he does stuff for the cops, and he comes to you and asks for what?"

"He wanted some information about a case. But it wasn't information I could give him. See, our information is pretty one way. He can bring me something he found out about the evidence I'm processing, right. But I can't tell him anything. I pretty much have to take it all straight to the prosecutor. But he said I was supposed to tell him, and he would tell Milford." Tony shrugged. "I told him that wasn't right, and I wasn't fucking doing it."

"And what did he do?"

"He left. But it was weird. And it left me thinking that Tammy had been pulling some seriously hinky shit for years with that dude and Milford."

"What did you do?" Mei asked.

"I went over my boss's head. That's what caused all the drama. That's when I got the hell out of there before I got fired."

"So you and Tammy being a couple had nothing to do with why you left?" Mei asked.

Tony barked out a laugh. "I told you, no. That was a stupid mistake. I wouldn't leave over that. It was because I tried to call her and Galen out."

Lemon sighed. "But I'm guessing it didn't matter, right? They got to keep their secrets and you were out."

"No, it sure didn't matter. I went to another prosecutor to tell them what I thought I knew. And they were basically like, look Milford Crane is untouchable. I can't do shit. Besides I didn't have any real proof. Which was true. I just wanted them to look into it, but they wouldn't. And that prosecutor called Tammy, and all hell broke loose."

"So, do you think Tammy and Milford could have conspired to kill Gaylen?" Mei asked. "Maybe because he turned on them or something. I mean, it sounds like he knew everything. He was right between the two of them, and he was with Tammy, then not with her. There's a lot of drama right there."

Tony shrugged. "I'm not gonna lie. I am no fan of any of them. But proving it. That's gonna be a bitch."

"So, let's say we think Milford Crane killed Gaylen," Mei said. Lemon's stomach churned. Another cat out of the bag. "But supposedly Crane has an alibi. How do we find out what that alibi is?"

Tony leaned over the counter, his gaze piercing Mei, then Lemon, then Mei again. "I don't know that. But I tell you this. If he did, his alibi is probably his co-conspirator."

"Aka Tammy," Mei said.

Tony sat back in his seat, nodding slowly.

Chapter Seventeen

Stephen Sikes slid a glass of Pinot Noir across the table, his lips puffed out in a perfect kissy face. "I am so happy to see you again, Lemon Lister."

Lemon glanced around frantically. Even though they'd chosen a quiet little bar off the beaten path, and despite Stephen's assurances that Milford Crane would never go there, she couldn't help but image him walking in at any moment, perfect suit lighting up the place. "Thanks for meeting me."

"When I gave you my number, I hoped you'd use it."

"Still trying to get my girlfriend out of jail. Just a reminder."

Stephen winked. "I know. And I came here to help in any way I could, just like I said I would the other night after you told me that horrible story about your girl being framed." He leaned over the glossy table between them. "But it doesn't mean I can't dream that she'll fall in love with some fabulous butch at the jail and you'll be all alone and need a shoulder to lean on. You know what I mean?"

Lemon ducked her head to hide both the flames on her cheeks and her shy smile. "I'll keep that in mind."

"Okay. So, what is it you need to ask me?" Stephen took a long swig from his own glass of wine.

Lemon peeked up at him, and to ease her nerves, took a drink herself. The smooth liquid slid down her throat and warmed her chest. She set down the glass and twirled the tall stem between her thumb and forefinger. "I heard that Milford Crane has an alibi for the time Galen Ryan was killed. And I'm trying to find out what that alibi is."

Stephen whistled. "Wow. You suspect him of killing Galen Ryan? Damn. I did not see that coming."

Lemon scrambled to prevent any damage her statement may have made. "I can explain."

"I mean, I figure there has to be something. Because putting innocent people in jail is a dick move I can totally see Milford doing, but murder is a whole other level, you know?"

Lemon took another sip of her wine and licked her lips. "So, like less than an hour before Galen died, I saw him at a dog park, not far from where, you know."

"No shit. You were basically there?"

"Yeah. And I saw Milford Crane. There at the dog park. With no dogs."

"Yeah, he hates dogs. But he knew Galen always went there." No surprise colored Stephen's tone, and that shocked the crap out of Lemon.

"Don't you think it's weird he was there right then?"

"Actually." Stephen took a drink of his wine and set the glass back down with a resounding ting. "I know about that. I mean, I didn't know you were there, of course. But I know about Galen and the dog park."

"Wait. You knew? You knew Milford was there just before Galen was killed?"

"Yeah. He was pretty freaked out about it, as I'm sure you were, too." Stephen reached across the table and took Lemon's hand, cradling it with both of his own. "Are you okay?"

"I mean, not really. But at the moment, I'm a little more concerned about Milford's alibi. I mean, I know I didn't kill Galen."

"He didn't either. I know because he was with me."

Lemon shook her head. "So confused."

"He went to the dog park to talk to Galen. I don't know what about, so don't ask. But I do know the convo didn't go so well. He texted me and said he was frustrated. Basically, he needed a booty call. He was at my house and in my bed before the shots were fired that night. I'm his alibi."

Lemon dropped back in her chair so hard the front feet left the floor for a second. "Damn."

"Sorry, sweetie. Didn't mean to burst your bubble. But if you want to commiserate with a bottle of whiskey back at my place, I can show you an approximation of what Milford and I did that night, with a few alterations of course." He wiggled his eyebrows while Lemon rolled her eyes.

****

"She says she'll give us fifteen minutes. Who the hell does that?"

Mei said. "I mean fifteen freaking minutes." Mei's hand quit flaying long enough to drop down into her lap, which was directly in front of where Lemon stood clinging to a strap dangling from the ceiling of the city bus.

"How did you even get her to agree to see us?" Lemon braced her knees as the bus hurled away from the curb and into traffic. Mei had shoved her onto it within minutes of Lemon arriving back from her evening dog walk. It wasn't until they were on their way that she even explained that they were headed on a last-minute visit to the crime lab to keep an appointment with Tammy.

"It wasn't me. I wish it was. It was Tony. I don't know what he told her, but the next thing I know, I get an email from her with Tony cc'd that says she'll meet me at six-thirty at the lab, and I can have fifteen minutes."

Lemon glanced at her watch. They might make it if traffic didn't screw them over. "Well did you ask Tony what he did?"

"I texted him. He said he told her I am working for Jade's defense team, and that it would look real bad if she didn't talk to me. He sent a winky face." Mei dropped her hands on her knees and rubbed her jeans. "My guess is that he used some of their bad blood to make a veiled threat."

"And it worked?"

"When you're guilty, you're scared."

The bus took a turn onto the street that held their ultimate destination. Only one more stop and they'd be jumping off. "So, what are we going to say? What are we going to do with our fifteen minutes?"

"Don't worry, my dear. While I was waiting for you to get home I talked to Andy. He gave me a list of questions and told me exactly how to ask them."

Lemon scanned Mei. She carried nothing with her, not a purse, bag, or folder. Her phone was shoved into her back pocket, her keys in the front. "Where is it?"

Mei tapped her temple. "It's all right here."

Lemon groaned. The bus jolted to a stop and the doors slammed open. A woman with three overloaded bags pushed past her to exit. Lemon might have considered snagging her seat, but with one stop left and a handful of other people also standing, she decided to stay put.

Mei glanced out the window behind her. "The bus will drop us off only two blocks away from the lab. Guess we'll have to huff it. Fifteen minutes. Seriously?"

The bus started up again, and Lemon swayed on her feet. "I think we're lucky we got any time at all. I mean, she didn't have to see us."

Mei turned back to glare at Lemon, her brows raised. "Oh, I'm pretty sure she did. If she's up to hinky shit and Tony knows about it, he has her right where we need her."

"But you heard him this afternoon, he's the one who lost his job when he tried to bring it up." Lemon bit her lip. "What if we're messing with really powerful people?"

"Oh, I'm sure we are." The bus curved into their stop and Mei stood. "Afterall, two people who messed with them are dead."

Even as the words hit Lemon, Mei sidestepped through the crowd to the door and leapt gracefully off the bus. Stuck in her thoughts, Lemon nearly missed the chance to exit.

She dropped onto the sidewalk just as the doors grabbed at her heel. Managing to stay upright, she quickly located Mei, five or six steps ahead. Lemon caught up to Mei just as she rounded a corner. "Hey, what do you mean?"

Mei didn't slow her pace. "About what?"

"Messing with powerful people and ending up dead."

"Well, it's what happened isn't it?"

"I suppose, maybe. But I was thinking," Lemon's stomach churned, "perhaps we should take that warning."

"Warning? Oh hey, here we are." Mei practically jogged to a large steel door and tugged on the giant handle. Nothing happened.

"Mei." Lemon pointed to her right where a rough-looking speaker perched off a steel pole at waist height. "I bet we use that."

"Hit the button," Mei instructed, not leaving her place at the door.

Lemon pressed the big black button. It left a sticky substance on her fingers. After a beat, a staticky voice spoke though, garbled and unintelligible. Whatever was said didn't seem to matter, because a second later there was a loud buzz and Mei yanked the door open.

Lemon hesitated. "This feels like the part of the horror movie where the audience is screaming at the idiots about to get killed."

Mei put her hand on Lemon's elbow and shoved her through the door. Lemon was plunged into a shining bright entryway, her eyes assaulted by the vast number of artificial lights stuffed into the boxy area.

A uniformed man stood inches away, his gaze pinned to them. "Who are you here for?"

"Tammy Ryder," Mei said.

Lemon reflected on the good fortune that Mei was able to talk, because she was terrified into silence.

Without a word of acknowledgement, the man turned and marched down the hallway ahead of them. He swiped a keycard on a pad and yanked open a wooden door. Mei scrambled to keep up, grabbing Lemon's wrist and pulling her along in her wake.

Just as she'd barely escaped the bus, Lemon barely made it through that security door. Without looking back to see the boisterous scramble, the man continued walking down the hall and made a sharp right turn. Mei and Lemon managed to get around the corner just as he stopped in front of a nondescript door and knocked on the wooden entrance.

He pushed the door open a crack as they approached. "Dr. Ryder. Your guests have arrived," he called into the room. Then he pushed the door open and stepped aside, holding out one arm, an inviting gesture that did not match the sour look on his face.

Mei spun into the room, still dragging Lemon, her claw-like hand gripped around Lemon's wrist. The hallway and non-descript door deceived Lemon into thinking she was entering a regular, ordinary, boring office. But this was a massive rectangular space stuffed with shelves and tables, each one overflowing with books, folders, metal instruments, scales, glass contraptions that looked like they walked out of a child's game of mousetrap. Pens and pencils draped over the whole mess like they'd been scattered by a confetti gun.

At the far end of the room, a woman sat behind a desk so clean and clear it contrasted with the rest of the room and demanded attention. Her short, bleached hair lay plastered to her head, the bangs nearly hitting a pair of dark, painted eyebrows. Her green eyes glared at Lemon and Mei as she rose and held out a hand over her bare, wooden desk. "You must be the person I emailed with earlier." She shook Mei's hand so fast she barely touched her. Instead of turning to Lemon, she gestured to two chairs opposite her.

Lemon had nearly tumbled over one of the boxy, brown chairs as they'd approached, so it was easy to flop down into it. Mei, far more graceful, lowered herself into the chair beside her.

"Dr. Ryder. It's a pleasure to meet you." The charismatic future museum curator that was Lemon's blunt and feisty best friend said. This face of Mei's, the one that got her a great job at a revered institution fresh out of college, could charm anyone into spilling their secrets. And Andy knew that when he'd set Mei on this course.

Tammy folded her hands together on top of the desk. "What, exactly, can I do for you?"

"We believe whole-heartedly in Jade Milan's innocence. As I'm sure you do, too. And we are working with her defense team to gather as much information as we can to support her case for release from any and all charges against her."

How Mei could be cursing out a teenager who spilled his flavored water on her on the bus and ten minutes later sound like she'd just passed the Bar, Lemon had no idea.

Tammy didn't move. Absolutely every fiber of her being remained still. Not an eyebrow raise, not a head shake. Nothing. "Of course. And how can I help?"

"What can you tell us about that day?"

"What day?" Tammy asked.

"The day Berkeley's body was found at the park." Mei's tone held no exasperation.

"What do you want to know?"

Mei paused to smile at Tammy. Lemon knew that little gesture was a lot more than it appeared to be. Mei was bringing up deep reserves of patience. "When did you see Jade that day?"

"I didn't see her until we were at the crime scene. She was off that day. She was helping search for Berkeley."

"She never came into the lab?"

"I didn't say that. I don't know if she came in or not. I didn't see her if she did. I saw her for the first time that day at the crime scene."

"But you didn't call her there?"

"No. She arrived on her own. I presume she was with an officer on a search when the call came in that we found the body."

Lemon had no idea what made her say what she did next. Maybe it was a newfound chip on her shoulder, or maybe she just wanted to see Tammy's reaction. "You mean when Milo found the body?"

Whatever the purpose had been, she didn't get any satisfaction out of Tammy. "I saw her at the same moment you did, I presume."

Lemon expected Mei to ask about Tammy identifying Jade's badge found near the body as the real one next, but she surprised her with a question out of left field. "Where were you the day Galen Ryan was killed?"

Despite her stillness, this question must have hit Tammy like a slap. Her head jerked back and her eyes widened. "Excuse me?"

"That's the other murder. The one Jade couldn't have committed. And I'm trying to determine what and who everyone might have seen that day. You know. Did you see anyone that was absent from the lab, or did you go somewhere and see something suspicious? Even the smallest thing, even if you think it's insignificant, can help."

Tammy's eyes narrowed. She went from shock and anger to suspicion with a tiny movement. But it was all written right there for Lemon to see. "I was at work before, during, and after that incident. I know nothing about it."

"I'm sorry for your loss."

Tammy's lips pressed together so tightly that if she didn't have a working nose she would surely suffocate. "Is there anything else? Or are we done here?"

Mei had completely blown it. They'd pissed Tammy off without getting any real information out of her.

"Lyka and Caroline." It was all Mei said. But something in the air changed.

Tammy sat back in her chair. "What about them?"

"I'm dating Caroline. And she watches Lyka sometimes." Mei hooked her thumb over her shoulder at Lemon.

"They are a gem. The police department is lucky to have them."

"Oh for sure. Caroline told me that she and Lyka have worked with your lab a lot to solve some a lot of interesting crimes." Suddenly, Mei the lawyer turned into gabbing fan girl. How did she do it?

"We have." A teeny tiny smile crept through Tammy's hard exterior.

"Can you tell me about some of them?" Mei's eyes widened, her hands splayed out on Tammy's immaculate desk. She literally looked like a tweenager about to see a K-pop band perform live.

Tammy leaned forward, her elbows resting on the desk. "Did she ever tell you about the serial peeping Tom we caught over in the Mission?"

"I feel like she said Lyka followed his trail, or something. But I can't remember the details."

"He did. Led to the guy two doors down from his latest victim. And we were able to match his DNA to the tree outside the window."

"Wait, what? Why was his DNA on a tree?"

Tammy lifted her eyebrows.

"Ewwww," Mei said. "Did he go to jail?"

"Oh yeah. He's there now. Then there was the woman who killed her husband. Did she tell you about that?"

"What? No!"

"Oh yeah. So this lady, Denise Myers, she claimed that her husband left for a bike ride at night and never came back, right. But they found him just one block from her house, massive head trauma. She says he must have been hit by a car. But Lyka followed her scent from the house to the spot where he was killed, and the lab matched his DNA to the business end of a baseball bat found in her garage. We got her, too. Milford got her life in prison for that little stunt."

Mei matched Tammy's posture, leaning over the desk toward the other woman. "Tell me more."

"Okay. How about this one. Milford's college girlfriend went missing ten years ago. As soon as Milford gets into the prosecutor's office, he vows he's going to find out who did it. His family had a private detective." Tammy paused, her eyes blinking quickly for a moment before plunging back into the story. "That, um, was working on it practically the whole time. And it was the PI who found the body. But my team, we figured out it had been moved from its original burial place."

"No way." Mei's eyes were as big as poker chips as she learned further over the desk.

"Yeah, so we gave Lyka this burlap sack we think was part of what was used to move the remains."

"Wait, did Lyka track the bag back to someone?"

"He did. Right there, in the police station, Lyka goes from sniffing this sack I'm holding out, down the hall, and into a room where a public defender is sitting with his client during a police interview. And the dog didn't go to the client. He went right to the public defender!"

"Wait. I did hear about this!"

"Didn't the public defender claim complete innocence?" Lemon said. "Like he didn't know her or something."

"Of course he claimed to be innocent." Tammy rolled her eyes. "But there's no way. And Milford got him convicted." She sat back in her chair. "We have a great team."

"But you're missing one member now, right?" Lemon said. "Jade."

Tammy turned her head slowly to move her kind gaze from Mei and pin Lemon with a harsh glare. "Yes. We are. I wish there was more I could do for her."

"Well there might be something," Mei said.

Tammy turned back to Mei and smiled. "What's that?"

"We think if we can find out who killed Gaylen Ryan, then we can find out who killed Berkeley."

"I don't follow." Tammy raised one thin eyebrow.

"The connection between the two murders was made by the police, not me."

Tammy pressed her lips together and gave a sharp nod. "Sure. Fine. But what does any of that have to do with me?"

"We're tracking down alibis for everyone who might have seen Gaylen Ryan that day. I mean, we're working with Jade's lawyer, so obviously we need to figure out how to clear Jade's mom, right?"

"Sure."

"And I don't know if you know this, but Milford Crane was seen with Gaylen that day."

Lemon tensed. She had yet to tell Mei and Andy what she'd learned from Stephen. There'd been no time. She went straight from meeting up with him at lunch to walking dogs, to the chaotic bus ride here. But she was still glad Mei asked the question. If Tammy alibied Milford too, then something was definitely up.

Tammy's eyes never moved from Mei's face, even though Lemon was pretty sure Tammy knew the witness from the dog park in question sat a few feet to her right. "I am aware."

"So, did you see Milford Crane that day? I mean, we know he isn't the killer, but we need to know who is. We just want to check him off the list, you know?" Mei cocked her head and smiled.

Tammy's chair emitted a creak as she leaned back, her hands dropping into her lap. "Sure. Sure. But I can't help you. I didn't see Milford that day. I'm sure one of his colleagues did at the prosecutor's officer. He's always working. I'm sure the police already have full knowledge of his whereabouts that day. You don't need to be worrying about this."

Lemon suppressed a sigh.

"Listen, I have to get back to work." Tammy rose. "But I appreciate that you are trying to help Jade. And I wish you all the best."

And just like that, it was over. Everything ventured. Nothing gained.

Chapter Eighteen

Sleep came hard that night. Lemon's mind reeled with all the possibilities. When she closed her eyes a web of people and connections appeared, stamped on the back of her eyelids. The spokes wove around Jade, Jade's boss, the boss's ex-lover (now dead), the boss's enemy turned Jade's business partner, the ambitious attorney tied to them all, and of course the canine officer and her dog with the broken sniffer.

By the time Lemon dragged herself to the van in the morning, a massive thermos of coffee in hand, she made a resolution. She slogged through town picking up the morning crew, and landed at the dog park with six rambunctious pups in tow.. She was going to get something out of that talk with Tammy. She was going to make it count.

She managed to snag a seat on the lone bench in the shade. The location, just beside the watering station, tended to be busy as dogs moved through, lapping up drinks and then loping away, mouths dripping water over her toes. Sandals were a dumb idea.

But she ignored all that and focused on her tablet. She still glanced up to check on the dogs. She wasn't irresponsible. But the words in front of her were riveting. One by one she looked up the cases Tammy regaled Mei with last night.

She scrolled through multiple articles on each case, ensuring she wasn't missing anything. But each one had the same three elements: the crime lab, Milford Crane, and Caroline and her dog Lyka.

The piece she couldn't figure out was who at the crime lab was involved in processing the evidence in each of the cases. No article, regardless of its obscurity or insanely in-depth reporting, mentioned the individual players at the crime lab. Though a few quoted Tammy as the head of the lab.

At this point she didn't know if Jade had been involved in any of these cases. Oscar the Chihuahua mix settled at her feet. She reached down to give him a pat. At eleven years old, he tended to run out of steam before the rest of the pack, all of whom were still playing hard.

She pulled up a notes app and jotted a few things down. Her memory was incredible. But she didn't want to miss anything. She'd have to get these cases to Jade to find out if she worked on them, and she couldn't afford to miss anything.

It was the last article about the last case Tammy mentioned—the one involving Milford Crane's college girlfriend, Tasha Mikels—that raised her pulse and caused her heart to beat faster.

Buried in a long explanation about the discovery of the remains and the determination that they had been moved was one tiny, but extremely important factoid.

"Officer Berkeley Hyatt, who attended the discovery, seemed unconvinced that the remains had been removed. She told our reporter that they appeared to be left where Tasha was killed."

Lemon stared at the screen. The yipping of playful dogs and the warmth of Oscar's small body covering her toes all registered somewhere in her subconscious. But the largest part of her brain became consumed with this thought: Berkeley was involved in the investigation of the murder of Tasha Mikels.

As her mind whirled, that piece of information gave way to a more frightening one: Berkeley doubted the lab's determination that the body was moved. And finally, the big dog daddy: the entire case rested on Lyka's determining that the body was moved by Nick Stephens, the man convicted of the crime.

Stillness gave way to frantic action as Lemon searched for Nick Stephens. Just as Tammy mentioned, Stephens was a public defender. One article listed all the clients he'd taken on in the three years between joining the office and being arrested for Tasha's murder. Lemon switched right back to still again, her thumb hovering over the screen as she read over the list. All of the other cases Tammy mentioned where Lyka and the lab and Milford Crane delivered justice had another common denominator—Nick Stephens defended every one of the suspects.

****

"Here. Here's the list. We need to ask Jade about every one of these." Lemon sent the text she referred to Andy. His phone, just inches away, resting on the table, buzzed.

"I can't see her today. They're on some kind of lockdown. I have to wait until tomorrow. Lemon, look at me." Andy tapped on the metal patio table.

Lemon's head shot up. She dropped her phone and met Andy's gaze.

"Take a breath, okay?"

Lemon pulled air into her lungs, filling them slowly. She exhaled just as slowly. "Okay."

"Where are the dogs?" Andy chuckled.

"I took them all home before meeting you."

"That didn't take long."

"They pretty much all live in Pac Heights."

Andy cocked up one lip. "Nice. Rich clientele, eh?"

"How do you think I make a living as a dog walker, dude." Lemon didn't mind taking a minute to banter with Andy. It helped calm her heartrate and her churning stomach.

She'd texted Andy to meet her the moment she put all the pieces together. He agreed to meet her at this café just a block away from where she'd dropped off her last client. Because she had such a big morning crew today she didn't have any of her own dogs with her. So now it was just her and Andy and the frisbee-sized metal table outside the café.

A server stopped to get their order. Andy got a black coffee and a cinnamon roll, explaining that he hadn't had breakfast yet, and he refused to be ashamed of his high-sugar diet. Lemon ordered a Latte and tried not to implode.

"Okay. Start at the beginning," Andy said after the server left.

"I don't even know where the start is."

"Well, I know you and Mei talked to Tammy Ryder last night, and I got a rundown from Mei in a massive text probably after you went to bed."

"Yeah, that sounds about right. So did she tell you about all these cases involving Milford Crane, the lab, and Caroline and her dog?"

"She did. She thought it was peculiar that the same three things were involved in all of the cases Tammy mentioned."

"Well so did I. So I did some digging into the cases today."

Andy put his finger and thumb perpendicular to one another and pointed at her. "I knew there was a reason I recruited you."

"Still don't have a paycheck, but yeah." Lemon flashed him a smile. "The thing is, it's weird right. They all have the same three elements involved?"

Andy shrugged. "Not really. The crime lab is going to be involved in everything the prosecutor does. Honestly, Lemon, there's no red flag there."

"What if I told you Berkeley disagreed with the crime lab on one of the cases. And not just any case, but the case of Milford Crane's murdered college girlfriend."

"I'm interested. Send me the link to the article."

"There's more." Lemon didn't bother picking up her phone. She'd already sent him the link. "The dog, Lyka."

"Right." Andy folded his hands together. "Tell me what you found out."

"He can't sniff."

Andy's eyebrows practically hit his hair line. "What?"

"I consulted with this dog trainer me and Zahn both know, Christina. And she tested the dog. And it was all weird, like I said. And so we took the dog to the vet. And he can't sniff. And don't get mad, but Zahn already knows. I planned to tell you all this, but I didn't want to text you because Mei knows how to unlock my phone, and she could have seen the text, and I didn't know what to do."

Andy gently touched her hand. "It's okay, Lemon. Calm down. Tell me everything you know."

"The dog literally can't smell. At least not well. Maybe better than you and me, but not compared to other dogs. And he definitely can't do the job he's been doing. Apparently, it's pretty sad. Poor dude. Did you know that a dog's sense of smell is like our sight?"

"That is sad. Are you telling me that the dog that solved all these crimes is a fake?"

"Yeah. I am. And Zahn knows. Am I in trouble?"

"Definitely not. Can I talk to this trainer? Christina?"

"Yeah. Sure."

The server returned with their drinks and a massive cinnamon roll, dripping with thick, white icing. When he was gone, Andy said, "Can you text her now?"

Lemon set down her Latte and scooped up her phone. "Oh, yeah, of course. Sorry."

She typed out a quick text to Christina asking if she was free. While she waited for a response she sipped on her Latte. Andy read through all the links Lemon sent, his brow furrowed, his fingers dripping with sticky icing as he tore off pieces of cinnamon bun and dropped them into his mouth.

It took a while, but eventually Christina responded. "Just got done with a client. Available now if you want to call.

Lemon glanced around at the other people perched at tables just feet away from them on the crowded café patio. "Andy. She's ready. Should we go somewhere else?"

Andy grabbed his coffee, threw some bills on the table and hustled away from the café. Lemon scrambled to follow him. He crossed the street and landed on a bench in a small city park, patting the space beside him. Lemon dropped down, and called Christina, hitting the speaker button as soon as her butt hit the wooden slats.

"Hello? Lemon?"

"Hi Christina. I'm here with my girlfriend's lawyer, Andy."

"Oh. Okay. What can I do for you both?"

"Well, the thing is. That dog we tested the other day, Lyka."

"Yeah?"

"He's responsible for some people getting prosecuted for murder."

A long, heavy pause punctuated the conversation.

"Really?"

"Yeah."

"That's bad."

"We think so."

A poof of air hit the phone line before Christina spoke again. "I'm kind of freaking out over here. What can I do?"

"To be honest, I'm not exactly sure. It was Andy's idea to call you. Andy?"

Andy smiled at Lemon before leaning over to speak into her phone. "Hi Christina. I'm Andy."

"Hi. How can I help?"

"What I want isn't too hard, I hope. I want to know what a real search dog would do, like how they work. And I need that on video."

"Okay," Christina said. "You want video of a search dog at work."

"Yes. With some commentary about how they do it."

"Okay. I don't have that, exactly. But there is a way we could get it."

"Yeah?" Andy's face lit up. "How quickly?"

Christina paused, causing Lemon's heart to skip a beat. "I'm free this afternoon, if Lemon can bring Milo."

"Milo?" Lemon asked.

"Yeah. I can't get ahold of a tracking dog on short notice. And my own dog isn't a tracker, just a searcher. At any rate, I need something specific, and Milo will do."

"But Milo isn't trained," Lemon protested.

"I don't say this often. And I don't want to be quoted. But Milo is a natural. I'll train him if you let me, so he can control when he tracks. But all the raw material is already there."

Lemon's sigh was so heavy that Christina laughed and Andy smiled. "Okay. When and where?"

****

Milo waddled along, his tail pointing at the sky, his nose grazing the ground. Lemon loved the big lug, but she had conflicting feelings about his nose. It was Milo who found Jillian's disembodied feet outside the Legion of Honor last year. It was Milo who tracked the scent to the rest of Jillian's body, and ultimately determined her killer.

And she was grateful. Really she was. But also, she wished they could just take a break from the whole smelling out dead people thing. Nevertheless, here they were. Milo panted noisily beside her. Andy and Christina stood in front of them both, expectant looks painted on their faces.

"Even though we don't have Lyka with us," Christina told Andy, "I have video of him. I can easily contrast the difference between a dog trained to follow commands about where he should go and how he should alert, and one who is actually using his nose to track."

Lemon stared down at Milo. He may have come to her by unconventional means, but he was hers now. They were family. She hated to put this much pressure on him. He was a sweet boy. Six years old. Quiet and easy-going, as long as he wasn't tracing the scent of a dead squirrel, he was a good dog, a great companion.

"Okay." Christina reached into her backpack and produced a metal container identical to the one she had used with Lyka a couple days before. "This has a scent in it." She hefted a twin metal container. "And this one holds an identical scent."

"What kind of scent?" Andy asked.

"In this case I used an essential oil. I wanted to replicate what Lyka did when he tracked the scent of the person who had supposedly moved the body in the case of the college girlfriend."

"I see. So not a cadaver?"

"No. Because that's not the premise of the cases in question. A dog should be able to do one or the other. In Milo's case, he can do both. And in Lyka's case he can't actually do either. Poor guy."

Andy wielded his phone, pointing it at poor, unsuspecting Milo. "Okay. The experiment is tracking a scent."

"Ready? Run this." Christina held out one of the metal containers and pointed to the mesh screen top. "With this open end facing down, along the grass all the way to the final destination. Then make sure the jar itself isn't visible when you hide it in the bushes."

Lemon dropped Milo's leash in Christina's free hand and took the container. She waited until she could hear Christina calling to Milo. Then she peeked over to see that Christina and a strategically held treat had his attention. When she was sure it was safe, she made a curvy route toward a set of thick bushes, dragging the container along the tops of the blades of grass as she went.

She hid the container among the low-hanging branches of the bush before quickly moving away and swiveling back to Christina, Milo, and Andy via a direct route, avoiding retracing her steps.

"Perfect," Christina said when Lemon returned, accepting a kiss from Milo as if she'd been gone from his presence for months instead of a few minutes. "Now we give him the scent to track. In a crime scene situation, we might have a piece of a person's clothing and we are asking the dog to track that person's path until we get to the person—which is represented by the other container. Make sense?"

Andy and Lemon both nodded. Christina smiled and turned back to Milo, presenting the other metal container. She gave him a command that might have meant something if he was trained. It was probably habit for her. But it didn't matter to Milo what random words humans said to him. He was ready to track. The minute he was done sniffing Christina's container, he stuck his nose to the grass-covered lawn and followed it with great diligence.

The three of them stayed put, watching closely as Milo moved across the grass. His heavy footfalls broke small twigs and disrupted chaotic piles of dried and crunchy leaves. He cared about none of it, his object clear, find the matching scent. He moved with purpose along the exact same path Lemon had taken. Lemon could have left a trail of cookies with every step for the accuracy it involved.

Milo reached the bushes and stopped. The gentle curve of his tail became a stiff flag. Dirt flew behind his paws as he dug them into the soil beneath the bush.

Christina hurried toward Milo, Lemon at her heels. "Does he usually dig when he finds something?"

"Yeah. He doesn't usually touch the dead thing, just digs around it. Like he's making it a little bed or something. Dude is seriously weird."

Christina reached the bushes and bent at the waist, peering in as she simultaneously tugged on Milo's harness. He obliged her, stepping back and plopping down at Lemon's feet.

"So he did it?" Andy asked.

Christina emerged from the bush, the metal container held up like a prize. "He sure did. And didn't damage the container at all. You were right, he dug around it." She glanced down at Milo. "What a good boy. Are you sure no one trained him before you got him?"

Lemon shrugged. "His owner isn't really available for me to ask."

"So." Andy held up his phone. "This is what would happen in a tracking situation?"

Christina faced the phone camera. "Yes. We gave a scent to look for. He found the scent's trail and followed it until he reached the scent in high concentration again. Then he alerted. Albeit in an unusual way."

"What's the other skill we need to see?" Andy asked, still holding the phone high.

"Cadaver." Christina said the word with an eerie cheerfulness and marched toward the bench holding her bag of goodies.

As they approached the innocent-looking pack, Lemon wondered how Christina was going to test Milo on cadaver scent. She silently asked the universe not to let Christina pull a body part out of her bag.

Lemon had quite enough of those for a lifetime.

To her great relief, Christina produced another innocuous metal container. This time, though, there was just one. "Okay. I'm going to have Andy place this one, because he is less likely to track you, Andy, then Lemon or even me. So, give me the phone."

As Andy and Christina made their exchange, Lemon emitted an audible sigh. She had no interest in being anywhere near that smell. Andy stared at the container, tipping it back and forth, and Lemon could see that this one did not have a mesh cover, but a nice solid one.

"Leave it closed. Walk one route to the hiding spot and different route back. When you get the final spot, you want to place the jar and crack it open. Don't take the top all the way off, just make sure the scent can get out."

"And hold my breath?" Andy said.

"No need. The scent is too subtle for your nose. Unless you stuck your nose all the way in that jar, you wouldn't smell it. Him on the other hand. He can smell it. And even though I didn't train him on this scent, we know he knows it." She spoke into the phone. "Twice he's found human remains without any commands or training."

Christina and Lemon took turns distracting Milo with cookies while Andy moved around the little clearing. Lemon purposely didn't pay any attention to Andy, just as Christina instructed. As a result, when Andy returned to the three of them, no one but him had a clue where he'd placed the jar.

Christina grinned. "This is the fun part." She rubbed her hands together.

Lemon, who still held onto Milo's leash held it up. "What do we do?"

Christina bent down and unclipped the leash from Milo's harness. "We let him do his thing."

For a few beats Milo just sat there, looking completely content to just hang out. But then his big, black, shiny nose moved. It was sort of like a wiggle. When she'd seen it in the past, Mei said it reminded her of Samantha on *Bewitched*. It happened a lot: at dinner time, when someone new came to the door, out on walks.

A second after that nose wiggle, Milo's legs popped into motion, following his nose again. This time he didn't stick to a trail, instead he moved back and forth like he'd had way too many glasses of wine, zig zagging across the lawn. "He's trying to find the strongest source of the scent," Christina explained. "Without a trail to follow he has to search for it."

When she wasn't attached to him via a leash, it was easy for Lemon to admire his work ethic. Instead of being careened through the park, trying to keep her footing while following the scent of some poor diseased squirrel, she could watch his low, muscular body, meandering tail, and floppy ears skim the ground as he worked.

"He's close," Andy whispered.

With Andy's phone held high, Christina said, "I can tell. See? He's speeding up. He's confident. The scent is stronger."

At the base of an olive tree, where a pile of leaves intertwined with long, wispy blades of grass, Milo stopped. His tail shot straight up and his paws dug into the leaves, sending them flying in all directions.

"Amazing!" Andy said.

"Incredible," Christina agreed.

"Milo," Lemon called.

Clearly dissatisfied with the little metal container, Milo turned and loped back toward her, big smiling jowls on display. God, she loved this little weirdo.

Christina retrieved her jar of death smell and shoved it back into her backpack. Andy stopped the recording on his phone, and Lemon hooked Milo back up to his leash.

"What now?" Lemon asked. Christina must have had the same question on her mind, because she tipped her head toward Andy.

Andy glanced up from his phone. "This will be useful later. But not yet. We have to find out who killed Berkeley first. That's what next."

Lemon's shoulders slumped. "How, exactly, are we going to do that?"

"I was kind of hoping he'd help." Andy pointed at Milo.

With the weight of the world on his long, sturdy back, Milo plopped down on the grass and sprawled out. Apparently, he was just as exhausted by all this as his mama.

Chapter Nineteen

"Thanks for coming everyone. I really appreciate it."

"Where the hell are we?" Mei looked around the wood paneled room with her nose wrinkled up.

"My partner, who bought out my firm, lets me use this conference room from time to time. You don't like it?"

Mei clearly did not. But Lemon was far less concerned about the décor than she was the company. Just hours after their adventure in the park with Milo and the dog trainer, they were packed around an oval table in this seventies-dream room with Jade's business partner, Tony, and a man Lemon had never seen before.

What were they doing here? That was the more pertinent question. It was also one no one had yet asked. It seemed that Tony and the stranger held the same trust in Andy as Lemon and Mei.

"Anyway, thanks for coming everyone. I have a few questions I need answered that neither Jade nor I can get to the bottom of. So, I thought we'd put our heads together on this.

Andy pulled on the cord of a massive white screen, the kind you used a projector with in 1992. It retracted up into a round puke-green holder attached to the ceiling. The action was accompanied by a cacophonous sound. With the screen out of the way, Andy revealed an actual chalk board. Like a green chalk board with little sticks of white, flakey chalk resting on a metal tray stuck to the bottom of it.

"Oh my god, Uncle. 1984 called and it wants its classroom back."

Andy ignored Mei. Instead, he picked up a piece of chalk and started writing on the board. The room full of people born in the late nineties and after sat in utter silence as the distinctive sound of chalk moving against slate swirled around them.

Eventually Andy turned around to reveal his masterpiece. Written in a triangle were the names Berkeley, Milford, and Galen. "We need to find the connections between these three people," he said. "What do we know?"

There was long, painful silence before Andy pointed to Lemon. "You first, Lemon. The one we know of right now is the Tasha Mickels case, right?"

"Yeah. Berkeley worked the case. Galen consulted on the case, and Milford prosecuted the case."

"Plus, Milford probably killed the victim," Mei said.

"Well, since we have no evidence of that," Andy said, "let's focus on what we know." He drew a line from Berkeley to Milford and wrote the words Tasha Mikels along the line. Then he drew another one from Milford to Galen with the same words. He pointed to the empty space between Galen and Berkeley "What we don't know in that case is if Galen and Berkeley had any contact over it, right?"

"Not that I could find," Lemon said.

"Anyone else?"

The room remained silent. So Andy continued, "Okay. Let's move on. What other cases do we have that would connect these individuals."

"Wait," Mei said. "Can we pause for a minute? Who's that?" She pointed to the stranger sitting across from Mei and beside Tony.

The person looked up at Mei, their bright blue eyes striking. Blond hair hug around their ears, and a shy smile painted their face. "I'm Hugo. Berkeley was my best friend."

"Wow. Okay. Well thanks for being here," Mei said.

"I don't think for one second that Jade had anything do with Berkeley's death. I want to get her cleared and find out who killed my friend."

"And we appreciate you being here," Andy said.

"Also, I know that Galen and Berkeley worked together on a case last year," Hugo said.

"Really?" Andy's eyebrows shot up. "Tell us what you know."

"Not too much. It came up because I'm Trans and Galen is Trans, and I was talking about Galen and what a role model he is in the community. She mentioned that she was working a case with him. All I know is that it was a robbery. I don't even know what the result was. I never asked." Hugo's lips turned down.

"Okay. Hugo says." Andy started to write on his board but turned around quickly. "Wait, Hugo, what're your pronouns?"

"He/his."

"Thanks." Andy turned back to the chalkboard, little white stick in hand. "He says that Galen and Berkeley," he drew a line between them, "worked on a robbery together last year." He wrote the word robbery.

"Does anyone know anything else about that case?"

Silence greeted Andy's question. He turned back to his small audience and leaned over the table. As the only person standing, it gave him an aura of power. "I need more."

"I got one," Tony said.

Andy stood up straight and pointed at Tony. "Shoot."

"They both testified on a case Milford Crane was prosecuting. I know because I was supposed to testify in that case, too. But it was right after I was fired, and of course, Milford decided not to call me. Anyway, Berkeley testified. She was the first officer on the scene. It was a murder. And Galen had been a consultant working on a profile before they had any suspects. I can't say they had direct contact in that case, but they both testified in court."

"That's good, real good." Andy made another set of lines on the board.

"But there's something else," Hugo said. "Something I haven't told anyone. I guess now is the time."

Andy turned around and dropped into the chair at the head of the table. Lemon, Mei, and Tony all leaned toward the wooden surface between them. Whatever Hugo was about to say was important. A sense of heavy intensity mixed with the thick anxiety in the air around them.

"So, um." Hugo scratched his nose. "I've been thinking about telling the police this, but I wasn't sure, you know. I kept waffling about it during the search for Berkeley. I was about to do it when they found her body and arrested Jade. I knew Jade didn't hurt Berkeley. And just the fact that they arrested her made me so suspect of the police. I just didn't know who to trust. But I feel like I can trust you all. You're here for the truth, no matter what. Right?"

"We are," Andy said.

Hugo took a deep breath, his chest arching out toward the table. "Three days before she disappeared, Berkeley told me that she didn't trust Milford Crane. She said he was up to something, and she knew it, but she wasn't sure what to do about it. I tried to get her to tell me what was going on. She was acting super cryptic about the whole thing. And she said there was no way she was involving me. She said she was sorry she brought it up, and that was it. I work for a social justice organization. And I admit that if you suspect law enforcement is up to something nefarious, I'm the last person you want to tell. But I'm her friend first and foremost. And she needed me." A tear sprung up in one of Hugo's blazing blue eyes. "I wish I could tell you more. But that's it. She changed the subject."

"That's good, Hugo," Andy said. "I can follow this lead. It's no problem."

Lemon hoped to hell that was true.

****

Lemon clutched the leather leash in her sweaty hands. Snickers didn't seem to care one way or the other. He was thrilled to be out and about with Mom for a little one-on-one time. Tongue lolling out of his mouth, the little fluffball smiled up at her. Lemon leaned over and stroked his chin. "Thanks for coming with me, buddy."

Snickers was the first of her three dogs she inherited. Adoption definitely wasn't the right word. Something had happened to the owners of all of Lemon's pups. But Snickers' story would always leave him with a special place in her heart. Not that she had a favorite. She totally didn't. But Snickers hadn't had alone time with his mom in a while. Also, his presence took the edge off.

It wasn't every day that Lemon received a request for a clandestine meeting with someone she'd never met. But here she was, sitting on a wooden slated bench in Jefferson Square Park waiting for exactly that.

Even though they were in the leash-free side of the park, Snickers was stuck to her side. He probably knew her unleashed anxiety could use a little support. As she scanned the park looking for the person whom she'd only seen in pictures, she ran through how the hell she'd gotten here.

Hayley's phone call came right after Mei left for work. Still sweaty from a rousing morning walk with a full slate of pups, Lemon had punched the button on her phone without even looking. Had Hayley been calling to find out why Mei and Lemon missed the last book club and if they were coming to the next? Lemon would not have been surprised. But what Hayley wanted shocked the shit out of her.

The instructions were specific: Meet up in a public place where you can talk without being overheard. Make sure no one is with you, especially not anyone involved in law enforcement, and that goes for lawyers, too.

Being in the middle of a scene from a spy novel did not make Lemon's bucket list. She'd contemplated calling Mei and telling her she had to take off work to help Lemon. But Mei had taken off enough days in the last week and a half to help with Jade's case. She had a big exhibit opening soon, and she simply had to work.

And Lemon had to find out what Felicia Kelly had to say.

She'd been so busy closely scrutinizing every person in the park that didn't have a dog, she completely missed the woman with the bouncy mini-doodle approaching from the right.

Felicia was sliding onto the opposite end of the bench and her little dog was giving Snickers' butt a thorough sniff before Lemon even realized what was happening.

"Hi Lemon. Thanks for meeting me."

Lemon smiled at the tall blonde and tried not to think of her pursuing Jade. Her sharp hazel eyes were surrounded in dark liner. Bits of purple glitter stuck to the area at their sides. Thick lashes, that could not possibly be real, batted above high cheekbones, and her full lips were painted in a shiny pink gloss.

But it was the rainbow halter top and super short shorts paired with three-inch wedge sandals that indicated Felicia was definitely in a whole different league than a dog walker in worn jeans and an old T-shirt with a youth softball team name splashed on the front.

The dogs, however, were more of a match. Snickers' past as the companion of a high-end businesswoman living in a remodeled Victorian in Pacific Heights showed in his demeanor and in the rhinestone collar his original mama had bought him that Lemon just couldn't stand to part with. He sniffed delicately toward the doodle.

"Yeah, um, I was pretty surprised when Hayley said you wanted to meet. And admittedly curious about all the…circumstances."

Felicia clutched perfectly manicured hands in her lap. "Sorry about all the weirdness. It's just that it's so messed up, and I don't know where to turn."

"Is this something you should be telling the cops instead of me?"

Felicia bit her lip. Lemon pinned her gaze on that spot where teeth met flesh, curious if it would ruin the lip gloss. But when she released her lip from the grip of her jaw, it was still perfect. How did that work?

"Here's the thing. I totally don't think Jade did this, and I want to help, and I'm gonna sound like a dick here, but I don't want to be a suspect again. I've been, when Berkely first went missing, and I can't do it again."

"I understand. And I don't blame you." Everything was coming into focus about this now. Felicia's best friend had explained all that she'd been through. Of course she was freaked out by coming forward with any new information, especially if she could be accused of keeping that information from the police before. In a way, maybe this move was super brave.

"Thank you. I appreciate that. I also want you to know that I am totally over my crush on Jade, really I am. I actually met someone while I was away from the Bay Area. She knows about all of it. She was the one who encouraged me to tell someone in a safe way if I could. So, I called Hayley and asked her to put us in touch."

"Is there something you remembered?"

"I'd be lying if I said I just remembered it. I knew it all along. I was just afraid to tell anyone. I actually tried to tell the police. But that didn't work out so well, and I stopped before I told them all of it."

Tension dripped off Felicia, and Lemon knew she needed to find a way to get her to tell the story without hyperventilating or running away. "Hey, maybe we should let the dogs play a bit, yeah?"

Air left Felicia's lungs in a loud whoosh. "Yeah. Pickles would love that."

They left the bench and moved into a grassy area marked by a perimeter of three tall, shady trees. "Go play," Lemon told Snickers. He seemed hesitant at first, but once Felicia released Pickles from the leash she was straining at, they were off.

Lemon smiled. "I love it when Snickers finds a friend. He usually won't play with bigger dogs. They have to be just the right size for him."

Felicia smiled and wiped her eye. "Yeah. Thank you. Pickles is only one, and she's so full of energy. I'm usually afraid to let her off leash unless there is another dog to focus on. She'll follow him completely, and he's clearly attached to you, so I suppose they're safe."

"Snickers will come when I call him."

"I guess you're kind of a puppy whisperer, huh?"

Lemon laughed. "Definitely not. But I did meet a real dog trainer recently, and those people can do some magic. I just got lucky in the dog department." Before Felicia could ask how she found her dogs, Lemon moved them back to the reason they were standing here in the shade watching dogs play. "So, what did you want to tell me?"

"Did you know that Berkely and I were friends?"

"I guess so, yeah. I think Jade said that's how you met."

"Berkeley and I went to school together. Anyway, Berkeley and me, we used to love to have picnics at Lake Merrit. We had a group of friends we'd invite that sort of changed with each event. But it was always the two of us, we were the organizers. We did it at least once a month when the weather was right. Sometimes I would invite people that Berkeley didn't know, and vice-versa. Jade came to one of the picnics."

Felicia ran a hand through her hair. "Anyway, this one time, Galen Ryan came. He was there on Berkeley's invite. She didn't really say how she knew him when she introduced us, and I didn't ask. Okay, so then another time, not long before Berkeley disappeared. Maybe a week or so, I can't remember exactly. But Berkeley told me that she and Galen were both involved in something scary. I asked her scary how, and she wouldn't say. But she had tears in her eyes. Then she started talking about how she loved me, and she needed me to know that. It was super sketchy and completely freaked me out."

A tingly lump formed in Lemon's throat. None of this could possibly be leading anywhere good. And she was completely unqualified to be hearing it.

Felicia didn't seem to think so, though. She continued with her story. "Then after that there was a night I was with Galen and Berkeley and a bunch of other people. It was after I was told to stay away from Jade, so she wasn't invited to this event. This was the night of Berkeley's disappearance. Anyway, Galen pulled me aside and said he had to talk to Jade and wanted to know if I knew how to get a hold of her. I asked him why he didn't ask Berkeley. It made no sense for him to ask me. And he said what he had to talk to Jade about something that he wanted to leave Berkeley out of. It kind of freaked me out."

"I would be freaked out, too," Lemon said. "I mean, what does that even mean?"

"No idea. But I left the party and went looking for Jade. I couldn't talk to Berkeley with Galen right there in the room. And I tried to text her, but she didn't react, so I figured her phone was on silent or something. Anyway, I tried to talk to Jade and that's when I got in trouble, and never did get to talk to Berkeley, and the rest is history."

"Wow. Damn."

"Yeah, and now Berkeley and Galen are dead, and Jade's in jail, and I'm terrified."

"I would be, too."

"What do you think I should do with this information?"

"I think we need to tell Jade's lawyer, at the very least."

Felicia's gaze landed on the two dogs, who were now running in circles after one another. "Okay. I suppose you'll set it up?"

"I will. I definitely will. But I think you should give me your number so we don't have go through Hayley again."

Felicia pulled out her phone. "Do me a favor, though?"

"Sure. What's that?" Lemon asked.

"Don't get murdered."

Chapter Twenty

Lemon had to rush home and get ready for the midday dog walk. She managed to get all the dogs in the car and on their way before she'd reached the outer limit of the timeframe she needed to operate in. The best thing in this circumstance was to go to a place she could easily park, walk them all without having to stop for lights at intersections, and get back in the van. She pulled out of the driveway of her last pick up and headed for Chrissy Field.

Whether it was her or Mei who'd left the radio in the van on she wasn't sure, and it might not have mattered if the news weren't so damn interesting. Lemon turned up the volume enough to hear over the clattering of the van on the road, but not enough to disturb the four large pups in the back bathing in air conditioning and lazing on thick foam cushions.

"We now join the press conference at City Hall. Prosecutor Milford Crane is going to be talking about the charges against crime lab employee, Jade Milan, in the death of Officer Berkeley Hyatt. Let's listen." The woman's smooth voice gave way to a booming, shouty, male voice. "I am more confident than ever that we have the right person in custody for Berkeley Hyatt's murder. And she is also a person of interest in the murder for hire of Galen Ryan. We believe the motive for these murders is jealously. We have uncovered a complex and tangled love triangle between Berkeley, Galen, and Jade. Turns out things got messy, and two of them ended up dead."

Lemon yanked the van into the nearest on-street parking spot and threw it into park. She couldn't safely drive when all she could see was red.

"We are not going to be taking any questions at this time, but would like to remind the public that neither of these killings is a hate crime, and the person ultimately responsible is in custody. Thank you for your time." Milford Crane's voice boomed through her car radio and straight into her heart.

Before she even cranked the key on the van to turn off the engine she had dialed Detective Zahn. He answered in two rings. "Zahn."

"It's Lemon. I'm pissed."

"I imagine you are."

"I have information I want to give to you."

"From where?"

"Felicia Kelly."

"When can you get here?"

****

It took Lemon exactly ninety-two minutes to get the dogs walked and all dropped back off at home, probably a new record. Five minutes after dropping off the last one she sat in a small room with Zahn.

"This looks like an interrogation room," she said as she plopped into an uncomfortable metal chair.

"It's an interview room. I understand this visit is official."

Lemon rubbed her forehead. Everything was getting very real, very fast. She had planned to have time to figure out exactly what to do with the information Felicia gave her this morning. At the very least she would tell Andy first. Sitting in an interview room that was most likely being videotaped with Zahn as stop number one was definitely not part of any plan.

"Look, Lemon." Zahn captured her attention from his seat across the table. "I know that Milford Crane's statement today was inflammatory."

"Inflammatory? It was utter bullshit! Completely made up bullshit with no basis in reality. The guy is literally just crafting a story to fit the narrative that suits him so he can blame Jade for both murders and not have to actually, you know, like solve the case."

"I know." Zahn pointed to his chest. "Believe me, I know."

"Do you?" Lemon cocked her head. A fire had been lit inside her when she heard that statement, and she couldn't quell it.

"Look. This guy is clearly desperate. He is trying to be the D.A. of San Francisco and he is so flummoxed by the stress of this case he just proposed a ridiculous scenario. And it will bite him in the ass. So? What do you have?"

Lemon bit her lip. What could she say about what Felicia told her? Now? Without thought or preparation? How could she protect Felicia?

Trading one innocent person behind bars for another didn't equal justice. And if she was trading Felicia for her girlfriend, what did that make Lemon? An awful person, that's what.

"I've heard more about the hinky shit this guy has done to rise through he ranks is all, and I want to know what you're going to do about it?"

Zahn folded his hands on the table between them. "I can't do a thing right now. I don't have a single piece of concrete evidence from a person willing to speak on the record that he did anything wrong."

"What about Tony Jillian?"

"A defense attorney could easily say that Tony is just getting back at his former employers. Sour grapes. I can't work with that. I need more."

That she didn't have. If Lemon told Zahn what Felicia said he could easily blow it off. As alarming as it was to her and Felicia, it was ultimately just supposition and intrigue. She didn't have a scrap of evidence to prove that both Galen and Berkeley had a reason to be afraid of Milford Crane.

"I don't know what I can do," Lemon said, the fire of conviction smothered inside her chest, creating a wafting cloud of smoke she nearly choked on.

"Well, there is one thing. I know it's a lot to ask, but I think it will help."

"What is it? I'm ready."

"Milford Crane wants to interview you himself."

Tendrils of cold ran up Lemon's spine. "What?"

"He's mentioned it before. But I told him you'd never consent, and since we have no reason to compel you, he didn't push it. But now I want you to do it."

"What? Why?"

"Because I will be in the room. I already negotiated that. And I want to watch. I think it will tell me things, things I need to know."

"But why does he want to interview me?"

"You're Jade's girlfriend, and he isn't satisfied with my conclusions that you don't know anything."

Lemon pointed to her chest. "I do, though. I know Jade didn't kill anybody, and Milford Crane is shady as shit."

Zahn brought one hand up to his mouth. She couldn't see most of his expression, but laugh lines formed around his eyes.

"Am I being taped right now?" Lemon looked around the room.

Zahn dropped his hand, serious expression on his face. "No. Not yet. But I will ask for your consent to be taped when we get Crane in here."

"Get him in here? As in right now?"

"Yes."

"Do I need a lawyer? Should I call Andy?"

"You can. But you are not under arrest, and this is not an interrogation."

"Yeah, I'm gonna call Andy." Lemon yanked her phone out of her pocket and sent Andy a text. *Milford Crane wants to interview me.*

Zahn stood. "I'm going to go track down Crane."

"Like, now?"

"Yeah. He's just down the hall in the room we use for press. Be right back."

NOW. Apparently.

A painful 30 seconds later, Andy responded. *I just got through security at the jail. Haven't seen Jade yet. Gotta ask her about the stuff we talked about. Can't come right now.*

Seriously? She was about to get interrogated by the man himself and Andy couldn't make it?

Kind of freaking out.

Andy replied faster this time. *Is Zahn going to be there?*

Yes.

Don't worry. It'll be fine. I will call as soon as I leave the jail. Good luck.

Good luck! A mild-mannered dog walker was up against a manipulative prosecutor and potentially cold-blooded murderer, and all Andy could say was good luck?

By the time Detective Zahn returned with Milford Crane, Lemon had made plans in her head for what she would do with the dogs if she spent the night in jail alongside Jade. Wouldn't they be a pair?

"Lemon. This is Prosecutor Crane," Zahn said casually, as if Lemon met murdering lawyers on the regular.

Crane took the seat directly opposite her. She expected Zahn to sit beside him at the small, square table. Instead, he moved around to site beside Lemon. This was new. The detective was sitting where a lawyer usually did.

If Crane noticed the strange configuration, he didn't say anything. He held his hand out to Lemon. "Nice to meet you, Miss Lister."

As she shook his hand, she stared into the same cold eyes she'd seen that day at the dog park, just before Galen Ryan was gunned down on a relatively quiet SOMA street. "Yes. What can I do for you?"

"Can you tell me about your relationship with Mei Lu?"

Lemon's mind whirled. Right up to those last two words she thought she knew what this was all about. But she was pretty sure he hadn't said: Tell me about your relationship with Jade Milan. No, he'd definitely said Mei Lu.

Lemon turned her head slowly toward Zahn. If she saw no surprise in his expression she would know this was a set up. She steeled herself for the possibility that she sat in the snake's den and was about to be eaten alive.

But when her gaze met Zahn's she saw matching shock there. There was no way this was a ruse or a trap cleverly orchestrated to paint Lemon into a corner. And if she had any doubt, Zahn placed one hand, palm down, on the table in front of her and leaned over toward Crane. "What is this about Crane? I thought you were going to ask her about Jade Milan, the woman you have in custody right now."

Crane flashed the detective a shit-eating grin. "I already know what I need to know about Jade. I'm interested in her accomplices."

"Whoa." Zahn held his hand out in front of him like a stop sign. He swiveled his head to look at Lemon. "You know what? I think you do need to get Andy here before we go any further."

Crane sneered. "Detective. I thought your job was to solve this crime."

"It is, but this isn't part of *my* investigation. This was a curtesy to you to interview someone directly related to the person you are planning to prosecute."

Crane turned away from Zahn and held Lemon's gaze. "Would you like to hear why I asked that question?"

"Yes." Lemon folded her hands together casually on the table, the way Detective Zahn had done earlier. Only she was pretty sure there would be bruises on the backs of her hands from her fingers digging into them.

"Good. I'm happy to share what I know. I understand you are familiar with Lyka. You were there when he found the body."

Lemon cleared her throat. If she was going to jail today—and it would most definitely be her because there was no way in hell she was saying a word to incriminate her best friend in anything—she was going to do it with style. "Actually, it was my dog, Milo, who found the body that day. Lyka was apparently struggling."

"Oh, right, yes. Well, he was there. And as you probably know Lyka has solved many cases for us. Anyway, we took him back to the site."

"When was this?" Lemon asked.

"Yesterday."

"I mean, it's definitely been a minute since the murder. What can he do now?"

"Oh, you'd be surprised what a dog's nose can do."

Lemon decided to let Christina be the definitive authority on that rather than this guy who prosecuted people based on the nose of a dog who couldn't smell. "I see."

"So Lyka tracked a trail from the body back to the location of the gun."

Lemon folded her arms over her chest, feeling downright cheeky now. "So the reverse of what Milo did the day he found the body, then."

"That's right," Zahn said. "Only I was unaware of this experiment." Fire flashed in his eyes as he glared at Crane.

"Yes, sorry about that. We needed to have some control factors, so no one that was there the day the body was found aside from Lyka and his handler participated in the experiment. At any rate, after Lyka went to the gun drop location, he continued on to another, third location."

Lemon ignored the growing pit in her stomach in exchange for taking on her badass persona—one she literally invented at that exact moment. "Interesting. And what location was that?"

"Well, it turns out it was the door of the museum. There the trail ends, for obvious reasons."

"So literally anyone that went to the museum all that week that Berkely was missing could have done it. That's a lot of people," Zahn said.

"Ah, but it was the employee entrance in the back. The one that leads to the break room. As it turns out, not very many people use that entrance. Only a handful that smoke or vape."

Lemon's entire body buzzed. What the hell was happening here? Was Mei being set up for a freaking murder by her current sort of, not really girlfriend? It made no sense. "Wait. I thought you were convinced that Jade committed the murder. So now you think it was Mei?"

Crane eyebrows rose, and she was sure she'd done something wrong. "Oh, I didn't say that."

Too afraid to glance over at Zahn, she pressed on. "What, exactly, are you saying?"

"Well, I think it's possible that someone close to Jade might have ditched the gun for her as a favor."

"Stop." Zahn held up his hand again. "The gun is not the murder weapon. As we know, as you've said publicly." He pointed his finger at Crane. "Berkeley was poisoned. Her service revolver was found without a single bullet fired."

"Oh, yes. For sure the moving of the service weapon was all part of a ruse of some sort. No doubt about that. The killer and her accomplice thought of everything. But they didn't count on Lyka."

"If they thought of everything. And if Jade is the killer, as you say, why would she leave her own work badge with the body?"

Crane ignored this question completely. "Did you happen to visit your friend Mei at the museum that day?"

Lemon's anger spiked, but only for a second. He was after her, not Mei. And that sucked, really sucked. It was exactly what she'd feared when she walked into this room without representation. But at least her mistakes wouldn't land her best friend in jail right next to her girlfriend.

"No."

"You sure?" Crane asked.

"I arrived at the museum that day, with Milo, when Detective Zahn called me. I was in the company of law enforcement the entire time, and I never went into the building."

Crane rubbed his chin. "What's your relationship with Jade, exactly?"

Lemon leaned back in her chair, arms tight across her chest. "Not answering."

"No?" Crane cocked his head. "Well, I already know you're on again off again lovers. What I want to know is if there were people in between, or even during."

Something strange enveloped Lemon. Whether she was channeling Mei or she'd actually become a different person in the face of this utter bullshit she didn't have time to fully analyze. But her anxiety fled in the face of the new suit of confidence she wore.

"That might be your bag, but it's not mine. I don't appreciate the assumption. Never assume."

Crane blinked. It took a moment for the politician to return. "Are you going to tell me about the nature of your relationship?"

"Why do you want to know?"

"I'm asking the questions here."

A sound emitted from Detective Zahn. Lemon glanced over at him. His lips were sealed shut, laugh lines sprung around his eyes. He stared straight ahead.

Lemon assumed she was doing well. She felt like she was doing well. And in that moment an idea sprang into her mind. She turned back to Crane. "Listen, it's complicated."

Crane leaned forward. Detective Zahn's gaze burned on Lemon's face. "Really?" Crane said. "Complicated how?"

Lemon ducked her head. "It's not something I'm comfortable talking about."

"Lemon, you must know how important this is. You want to help, don't you?" Crane's tone suddenly turned sickly sweet.

"I do, but...do you think I could write it down?"

"Of course." Crane looked up at the ceiling. "I need a pen and paper, stat," he commanded.

Lemon kept her gaze trained on the table between them, unsure if this new being overtaking her body was capable of keeping secrets with her eyes. Eventually, an officer skipped into the room, dropping a pad of paper and a cheap pen on the table in front of Crane.

"Here you go." Crane slid the pen and paper across the table toward Lemon.

Lemon tucked the pad into her chest, curving around the paper as a left-hander does. She wrote five words before frantically shaking the pen. She set it to the paper again, then glared at the offending writing utensil. She shook it again, pressed it to the paper once again, then tossed it into the center of the table. "I need another pen."

Crane immediately reached into the pocket of his button-up shirt and pulled out one of the three pens stacked there. All identical. All high-end. Lemon noticed them the moment he entered the room.

"Thanks." Lemon touched the pen's clicker with the tip of her thumb nail and carefully held the pen with just the tips of her fingers, making sure not to contact the large rubber comfort grip.

Silence blanketed the room save for the slow movement of Lemon's hand over the paper and the whisper-soft travel of the pen. Lemon dragged it out slowly, partly because she had to make up what she wrote as she went and partly to achieve her desired outcome.

Walking the line between providing something to satisfy Crane enough to let her leave without accidentally giving him something he could use against Jade, Mei, or herself wasn't easy. She ended up writing a long, convoluted explanation about how she'd always been monogamous. She went into great detail about that. Then she related the story of a friend who was polyamorous and talked about how much she respected that as well but didn't think it was for her. But then again, queerness was complex.

She spent at least three pages of notepaper exploring what might or might not be Jade's opinion on polyamory, ultimately ending in ambiguity. By the time she reached page eleven of her manuscript she'd said absolutely nothing, and as she predicted, had Crane at the end of his patience rope.

She glanced up at him and held out the papers. Crane kept his eyes on the long diatribe, his focus there complete, allowing Lemon to perform a slight of hand her card trick-loving grandfather would have been proud of. "Can I go now?"

Crane accepted the notepad greedily. "I'll need to review it first."

"Wait a minute." Lemon stood. "I thought this was a voluntary interview." She waved one hand wildly. "And Detective Zahn said I didn't need my lawyer. But maybe I do."

Crane stood, holding one hand out in front of him. "Hold on, Lemon. Now, just calm down."

"I will not. Am I free to go or not?"

Crane's Adam's apple bobbed. He glanced longingly at her long diatribe gripped in his hands. "You can go."

"I'll walk you out," Zahn said.

And just like that Lemon left, with Milford Crane's pen tucked discretely into her pocket.

Chapter Twenty-one

Lemon gripped the plastic bag—the only one she could find in their entire apartment—in her left hand. In her right, Milo's leash chafed her palm.

"Is this really going to work?" Mei asked. There was no attitude behind her question. Just the sheer terror that still lingered following Lemon's recounting of her meeting with Milford Crane a few hours earlier.

"Chances are good. It hasn't rained, and a good tracking dog can pick up a scent as many as 14 days after the trail was laid. And he's very good."

Milo lay at Lemon's feet. Unimpressed with this whole set up, he dropped his chin onto his paws, his big ears folding over themselves like a blanket discarded carelessly on the floor.

Lemon glanced around and shivered. She stood in this exact spot a week and half ago, and moments later her entire world had shifted. Now they were here again, hoping to shift it all back, or at least move it in another direction.

Andy and Zahn looked strange standing beside each other, creating a block in the aisle between the bushes. They just finished a rousing show and tell, identifying the exact spot where Berkeley's service weapon had been found. Now they both stood on the opposite side of that little patch of ground from Christina, Mei, Lemon, and Milo. Both held expressions of excitement. In fact, Zahn looked more animated than Lemon could ever even have imagined the stoic detective appearing.

"What do I do?" Lemon asked.

Christina held out her hand. "May I?"

Lemon let out a massive sigh of relief as she handed the plastic bag over to Christina. "Please."

Christina didn't immediately unveil the object inside. Instead, she pulled a treat out of a pouch attached to her hip and called Milo to her.

Lemon let go of his leash, her hand aching as her fist unclenched. Milo trotted over to Christina. She gave him a treat and then picked up his leash. "Good boy, Milo. Now I need you to do something else."

Christina looped the handle of the leash over her wrist and used both hands to pull the pen most of the way out of the plastic bag. She folded the bag over her arm, ensuring that just the writing end of the pen encased in the plastic, leaving the end most often touched by human hands open.

She lowered the pen toward Milo's nose. She didn't need to give the big hound a command. When presented with the object he immediately leaned forward, stretching out his neck, the big wrinkle below it swinging slowly. His big, black nose quivered.

Then, he stuck his nose to the ground and began to move. Without words, Milo's audience seemed to understand their role in this play. They moved away from the dog and Christina, bumbling into the bushes to get out of his way. Lemon ended up wedged between something with soft, dewy leaves and something hard and spikey. Her shins trapped in this dichotomy, she kept her gaze on Milo.

Mei, Lemon, Andy, and Zahn created a large, loose circle around the area where the gun was found. All eyes floated between the dog and the spot, the dog and the spot. But Milo just kept moving in erratic circles.

After a good ten minutes, Milo stopped, sat down, and stared up and Christina. She gave him a treat and patted his head. "Good boy."

"Good boy. He didn't even get to the spot," Zahn said, frustration clear in his tone.

"No. He told me he hasn't found the scent. But just wait. We'll try one more thing." Christina smiled making it clear she was the calmest person standing outside the de Young Museum at that moment.

Christina led Milo to the exact spot Mei had stumbled across the gun while hiding her vaping habit from her co-workers. She pointed to the ground at her feet. Milo sniffed at it diligently, moved around it, even bumped into a bush. But in the end he sat at Christina's feet and stared up her, his mission not accomplished.

"I'm afraid Milford Crane's scent isn't here."

"But he was here," Lemon said. "He told me he was here with Caroline and Lyka. They followed the scent from the gun to the employee entrance." Lemon pointed to the innocuous metal door behind them.

Christina's brows knitted then dropped. "Okay. Let's go over there."

Milo loped casually beside Christina as they headed toward the open grassy area behind the employee service door. Their nervous audience followed at a careful distance, still in a loose semi-circle formation.

Almost as soon as they left the bushy area and hit the open grass between the building and the wild overgrowth, Milo's demeanor changed. His nose hit the ground, his legs picked up the pace. Christina's slow walk turned into in a faster canter. She kept up with every one of his moves, keeping the leash loose so it wouldn't pull on Milo.

The big dog took a purposeful track in an almost straight-diagonal to the employee service door. When he reached the door he stopped, tail in the air. Christina praised Milo and gave him a treat before turning to everyone else.

"What does that mean?" Andy asked.

Christina didn't immediately answer him. Instead, she turned to Zahn. "Did you see a video of Lyka finding the trail from the gun to the door?"

"Yes."

"Tell me what—exactly—was on the video."

"The video starts back there." Zahn pointed to the edge of the trees. "About, no, exactly where Milo started sniffing and went to the door."

"So the video didn't actually show Lyka in the bushes at the location of the gun?"

Zahn shook his head. "I did ask about that. They said it didn't matter. It was tossing distance."

Lemon kept her scream internal, somehow, but Mei growled.

"Well, I will tell you what I know," Christina said. "I know there is no way Lyka can track a scent at all, let alone days later. I also know that Milo can. And he just did. Your D.A. was here and followed this route, probably following Lyka. But he didn't place that gun."

"Couldn't he have tossed it?" Mei asked. "Takes one to know one, right?"

"It's too far," Zahn said.

"I agree," Christina said.

"Definitely," Andy said.

Lemon, who was notoriously bad at estimated distances wasn't about to argue. "So, he's not the killer?"

"He didn't put the gun here," Christina said.

Zahn asked, "Is there any point in seeing if his scent is at the body dump?"

"We can check it out. But Milo specifically tracked the gun back to the dump site. So unless you have two people involved," Christina shrugged. "I guess we can check."

Zahn gestured with his hand. "Let's go then."

After another 30 minutes, Milo lay over Christina's shoes sound asleep and all the humans stood at the base of the body dump hill and stared at each other.

"I'm sorry. But Milford Crane hasn't been here."

Mei stared down at the dog. "Milo, dude. You gotta help us out here." Milo lifted his head and stared at her. She let out a frustrated groan. "I wish you could talk." Milo stretched his head in her direction.

Lemon noticed the subtle twitching of his nose just before he rose and trotted over to Mei. He stretched his head so he was able to touch the tail of her shirt, a button-up in baby blue Lemon didn't remember ever seeing before. "What's he doing?" Mei asked, her body completely still. Despite living with three dogs, her lifelong fear of canines sprang to the forefront with this kind of scrutiny by a sixty-five pound hound.

"He's smelling your shirt."

As soon as Christina had the words out of her mouth, Milo moved away from Mei, nose planted to the ground. His tail stuck up in the air, he moved across the grass, away from the mess of vegetation where Berkeley's body had been dumped, down the hill, and toward the picnic area.

Lemon remembered him pulling her past this area when he was following the track of the scent from the gun. He blew past families eating sandwiches, bypassing the area altogether on his way to Berkeley's body.

But now Milo was completely engrossed in one picnic table in particular. For a moment Lemon feared that he was just looking for a dropped morsel of hamburger or tuna sandwich. The embarrassment was already creeping up on her when Milo pivoted completely.

Christina followed Milo easily as headed in a straight line from the picnic table, up the hill, toward the body dump site. His posse followed as well, both Andy and Zahn holding their phones up to capture Milo's quest.

He landed in the exact location of the body. But now his demeanor changed. He smelled death. Tail straight up, vibrating quickly, he began to scratch. Christina pulled him away from the site, out of the bushes, and back down the hill. She got him settled on the grass with a handful of treats.

"I am not sure I understand," Mei said. "I mean. I was here that day. So is he saying that I was here. Because, we already know that."

"You never went to the picnic area." Lemon pointed to the table Milo led them to. "Never. There was a family there that day eating and we never went anywhere near them."

"Are you sure about that?" Zahn asked, turning his phone toward Lemon.

"She's sure," Mei said. "Her memory is crazy good." She tapped her temple.

"Christina, what does all this mean?" Andy asked.

Christina turned to Mei. "I don't know. Why would he sniff you then go to a place you've never been?"

Mei shrugged. But as soon as her shoulders hit her ears she paused, stuck in a frozen moment. Then her shoulders dropped and her eyes grew wide. "This isn't my shirt."

"Wait," Lemon said. "I knew it was new."

"No. It's not mine at all. I just grabbed it and put it on for work today because I had a meeting with a donor and I needed something a little nicer than my usual polo."

"Grabbed it from where?" Andy asked.

"Lemon's closet?" Zahn asked.

Lemon contemplated tossing him a dirty look, but didn't make it that far because Mei answered the question. "No. It's Caroline's." The tone of Mei's voice matched the slump in her shoulders. "It's Caroline's shirt."

Christina took a step toward Mei. "Was it washed before you wore it."

"No. It wasn't."

Christina let out a long breath. "I think you need to take it off. Now."

****

Surrounded by cops wasn't the best way to have a heart to heart, but Lemon had no choice but to check in with Mei. They stood side by side on the street. Rows of Victorian houses loomed over them, their judgement clear.

Mei stared down at the orange shirt covering her torso. "Did they have to give me this? Seriously?"

Lemon couldn't help but think that the police officer who pulled the shirt out of her trunk to replace the borrowed button-up might have tried harder to come up with something that didn't make Mei look like she'd escaped from San Quinten.

Standing on the street where Galen Ryan was killed, surrounded by SFPD, Mei definitely looked like a prisoner who'd been brought by the detectives to the scene of the crime. It was straight out of a *Dateline* episode.

The borrowed shirt was held in a plastic bag clutched in Christina's hands not far away. She and Milo waited patiently for the police to set up a camera and mark locations with colors Christina assured them wouldn't mean much to Milo if he did actually use his eyes instead of his nose—which she said was highly unlikely.

"My dog is implicating your girlfriend in a crime. And I think we should talk about it," Lemon said.

"I told you before, she's not my girlfriend." Mei kept her gaze on the dog in question. "It's only been a little over a week, and I was thinking of calling it all off anyway." Mei turned to Lemon. "Really. I promise. I'm okay."

Lemon touched Mei's arm. "Really?"

Mei covered her hand with her own. "Really. Honestly, it sucks. But Jade shouldn't be in jail and Berkely shouldn't be dead." A tear dropped out of her left eye. "And if Caroline had something to do with it, I want her ass in jail."

Lemon hugged her best friend, squeezing her tight.

"Ladies," Andy called. "Look."

He pointed straight at Milo. Lemon's dog sniffed the shirt Christina held and immediately stuck his nose to the street. He followed the scent to the exact location marked by the police as the place where the shooter most likely stood when they killed Gaylen Ryan, then a few steps toward the mark where the body lay dead, then back again toward the curb, where he stopped and sat down.

"Well I'll be damned." Zahn called to the officers in the street. "What do we have on those cars? Anything?"

"Yes, detective," one responded. "One of the neighbor's security cameras shows a car right here leaving immediately after the crime."

"The red compact. I know," Zahn said. "But we couldn't get a license plate. That car was right here?" He pointed to the spot Milo had stopped.

"Yes, sir," the officer called back.

"Wait!" Mei moved toward Zahn, her arm in the air. "Did you say a red compact?"

Zahn's gaze stayed with Mei, who stood in her criminal garb. "Yes."

"Did it have a dent in the hood, right near the front. A long line, like it hit the bumper of a trailer?"

Zahn cocked his head. "Does it?" he asked the police officer to his right.

She looked down at a tablet in her hand. Then brandished it toward Mei. "I think so."

Mei stared at the tablet. Then she stepped back. Lemon caught her. "Yeah. That's Caroline's car."

Chapter Twenty-two

Zahn had warned them it might take a while before Jade was released. But Andy, Lemon, and Mei were willing to wait.

"Please tell me the Milan's aren't on their way." Mei stretched her arms over her head before slumping back into the uncomfortable chair in the waiting room of the county jail.

Andy chuckled, briefly interrupting his job of scratching Milo's chin. "No. I told them I would bring her to them first thing in the morning, and they agreed to stay put."

"Well, that's one small miracle, I guess."

Lemon glanced over at Mei. Her dog-fearing best friend kept her gaze stuck on Milo. "I'm so sorry, Mei."

Mei waved her hand.

"Are you mad at him?"

Mei lifted her head to look at Lemon. "Milo? No. Grateful, actually. He saved me from a big mistake. I mean, I don't think it was going anywhere, but what if it did? She's a freaking cold-blooded murderer." A tear dropped down Mei's cheek. Lemon's heart squeezed.

Mei leaned over and, for the first time ever, gave Milo a soft stroke on the top of his head. "Thanks, dude."

Milo stuck out his long tongue and swiped it across her wrist.

Lemon turned away from the moment and forced herself to speak. "Andy, what do you think happened?"

Andy cleared his throat. "I've got a pretty good theory. It will be a while before the police confirm it, but I think I know what happened."

Mei, her hand still on Milo, looked at her uncle. "Well, go on. Tell us."

"Caroline, Gaylen, and Milford were running an evidence racket."

"Oh for sure. And Tammy, too, don't forget," Mei said.

"Hmmm. I'm pretty sure you're right. Though her part may be harder to prove. At any rate. The trio, along with help from poor, unsuspecting Lyka, planted or created evidence against suspects to help Milford Crane get high-profile convictions. And in at least one case, to pull the scent off himself."

"The dead ex-girlfriend," Lemon said.

"Yes. That one is going to require a lot more investigation. But, anyway. They were all working together."

"And doing hinky shit," Mei said.

"Definitely."

"And Berkeley?" Lemon asked.

"I think she found out about it. And I think she talked to Gaylen about it. And maybe Gaylen had a change of heart. I don't know, but I'm pretty sure that the two of them were going to expose the evidence-altering ring."

Mei's shoulders dropped. "So Caroline decided to kill Berkeley?"

"To be honest, I'm not sure how premeditated it was. It's possible they met at the park to talk about it. Or maybe, Berkeley was at the park on patrol and Caroline met her there. Not sure at this point, because the police aren't talking. But either way, I think they ended up at that picnic table talking. And Caroline offered Berkeley a poisoned drink."

Lemon pointed her finger at Andy. "That's premeditation."

"Probably. As a defense attorney, I would say that she brought the poison to the party but hoped she could talk Berkeley into playing ball and not having to use it. Not saying it would work, but that's what I would try. Anyway, she poisoned her and then dragged her body into the bushes."

"And the gun?" Lemon asked.

"My guess is that she planted it on purpose to use it, along with Lyka, to steer the investigation in the way she wanted to. Maybe she didn't know what to do the day Mei found the gun. Maybe Mei found it too early. Perhaps Caroline was hoping the body would stay hidden longer as well as the gun. At any rate, she didn't give Lyka clear instructions on what to do, and Zahn called on Milo." Andy reached down and gave one of Milo's big ears a long stroke. "And that changed everything."

"What about Jade's ID?" Mei asked. "And Jade's sweatshirt found in Berkeley's trunk."

"Oh, I think Caroline planned to frame Jade from the beginning. She placed the ID Card there. According to Jade, she could have gotten the sweatshirt she planted in Berkeley's trunk from her locker at the same time. And she probably planned to have Lyka lead back to the body from the gun so the police could find the ID, but something went wrong."

"I bet it was too far to get him to follow her directions. I mean, it was all the way across the park," Lemon said.

"We'll ask Christina what she thinks," Andy said. "But yeah. Definitely a possibility."

Mei rested her hands on her hips. "So Tammy must be in on it. She had to be the one who created the fake ID."

"It's a possibility. We'll see what they can prove. There's also Marla's necklace to deal with."

"Oh," Mei said. "That the unknown police officer swiped from the pawn shop and planted with Galen's body."

"Yes. I suspect that was Caroline herself. Meaning she planned Galen's murder in advance for sure."

"And she planned to frame Jade's mom for it."

"It was probably the easiest way. Caroline called Marla the day Jade was arrested and asked if she could do anything to help. Marla didn't remember exactly what she told her. She admits to being a bit hysterical." Andy flashed a wry grin. "But she probably told Caroline she was pawning jewelry to help with Jade's expenses. It wouldn't be hard to find the right pawn shop in San Rafael and steal something of Marla's to plant at the crime scene."

"Then she followed Gaylen and killed him?" Mei asked.

"Oh, I'm not so sure Milford didn't make sure Gaylen was in the right place at the right time, if you know what I mean."

"But broad daylight in the city? It just seems so risky."

Andy rubbed his chin. "Maybe not. It's obvious, meaning a cop wouldn't possibly try to pull it off, but an inexperienced person trying to help Jade, sure. Besides, only one camera on that entire block worked that day, who else would even know that?"

"How would anyone know that?" Lemon asked.

Andy just smirked. "Anyway, this is a convoluted case. But I'm going to keep my eye on it."

Mei leaned over, wrapping her arms around him. "I'm so thankful, Uncle!"

Lemon draped herself over him on the other side. "Me, too."

"Okay. Okay. Stop now. I gotta go check on our prisoner."

****

Despite her face being a disturbing shade of pale, Jade's lips were planted in a soft smile. "I don't even know where to start to thank you."

Mei, busy at the stove, must have thought she was talking to her and Lemon. "Don't worry about it."

Lemon chuckled. "She wasn't talking to us."

Mei turned away from the pan. Her gaze moved across the dining area until she located Jade sprawled out on the floor in front of Milo.

"Yes, sweet boy. I owe it all to you," Jade told the hound.

"So much for the humans who worked night and day," Mei grumbled before turning back to the stove. "Dinner's ready, by the way."

Lemon set the table. Jade poured the wine. Mei served the food.

When they'd put a dent in the stir fry, they finally turned to the elephant in the room. It was Jade who started their plunge into the darkness. "I've been reinstated."

"Yeah. Already?" Lemon asked.

Less than a week had passed since they watched Jade walk out of the jail early in the morning after Milo's nose hunted down the real killer. After a few hugs, they'd delivered Jade to her parents' house, where she'd stayed until the press settled down. Tonight was her first return to the city, and they were celebrating with a quiet, slightly somber dinner.

"Yeah. I got a call from the new director this morning. He said to take my time coming back, though. I'll probably wait at least another week. But I'm looking forward to going back to work."

"New director?" Mei asked.

Jade dropped her fork and smiled. "Tammy has been removed."

"She should be in jail," Lemon said.

Jade took a sip of wine. "All in good time. Caroline is singing like a canary from what I hear."

"That's what Uncle Andy said as well," Mei swirled her wine glass. "He said he thinks she's trying to get a better deal for herself by telling all on Milford Crane and Tammy Ryder."

"You think it will work?" Lemon asked.

"No," Jade said. "I don't think so. You don't get to kill two people—one of them a cop—and get off easy." Her gaze flitted to Mei. "Sorry."

"Don't do that," Mei said. "I'm over it. I'm happy she's in jail and you're not." Mei stood. "Speaking of which, I'm taking these dogs for a walk so you two can catch up." She stood from her seat.

"Wait. What?" Lemon asked. "You're taking the dogs for a walk?"

"Yes. Don't act so surprised. I've done it before." Mei scanned the three pups, all staring at back at her from their cozy perches on their beds. "But one at a time. I think that's still best."

"Take Klee first. He's the easiest to walk. He'll just stay by your side and doesn't get distracted by smells like Milo."

"Okay." Mei slid over to the hanging rack full of harnesses and leashes. Her hands hovered over them one at a time. "I think I tried to put Milo's leash on Klee last time. That didn't work so well."

"The orange one," Lemon said.

Mei snatched up the orange harness and leash set, dropped to a squat, and held the whole contraption out to Klee.

"Hey," Jade said. "Speaking of dogs. What happened to poor Lyka?"

"It's a good story, tell her, Lemon. Come here Klee." The little dog trotted over to Mei obediently and waited with great patience as she fumbled with the clasps.

Mei managed to get Klee hooked up, then rose and slipped out the door with a sloppy wave.

Jade turned back to Lemon. "So what happened to Lyka?"

"The police department officially retired him. Christina, the dog trainer, adopted him. She's going to get him certified to be a therapy dog. He'll start a new career working in hospitals and helping people heal."

"That's beautiful." Jade wiped at her eye.

"Are you really okay?"

Jade's answering smile was soft. "I'm doing pretty good, honestly. It's amazing what freedom can do for your spirits."

"Listen, Jade. When you were gone, I realized how dumb it was that we weren't together. I mean, it was just…it was dumb."

Jade cocked her head. "I really missed you. Both before jail, and, you know, during. When Andy told me about the plane tickets Caroline purchased in our names, I kept thinking about how nice it would be to go on a vacation, sit on the beach, and drink Margaritas. The daydream got me out of that cell for a little while, at least in my head."

Lemon dropped her hand onto Jade's knee. "Watching you go through that, it really, really hurt. It was awful. And I realized...you know."

Jade leaned forward. "Yeah, Lemon. I do know."

And then they were kissing, and everything else melted away. The murder. The set-up. The time in jail. The stress of the investigation. Mei's girlfriend being a homicidal maniac. It all disappeared behind that happy little wall that was the safe place where Lemon and Jade came together.

THE END

Author Bio

Benna Bos lives in the iconic city of San Francisco with her spouse and her dog. She enjoys placing her characters in this foggy setting and creating stories that weave in the landscape she has come to love. She is obsessed with true crime podcasts, dogs, and museums. Somehow she's lucky enough to get to write about them all.

Books by Benna Bos

Lemon Lister Mystery Series:

Murder At the Museum

Murder By the Bay Mystery Series

Investigating Helen
Defending Jessica

Bringing rainbow stories to life.
Flashpoint Publications welcomes submissions from writers of every color and books featuring characters of every color. In addition, Flashpoint Publications encourages job applicants of every color whenever a staff position becomes available. We believe that EVERYONE is entitled to a seat at our table.

www.flashpointpublications.com

www.ingramcontent.com/pod-product-compliance
Lightning Source LLC
Chambersburg PA
CBHW070654100726
47907CB00007B/2201